SLAM DUNK

THE #1
SPORTS SERIES
FOR KIDS

SLAM DUNK

Text by Robert Hirschfeld

LITTLE, BROWN AND COMPANY
Books for Young Readers
New York   Boston

For my great-grandson, Travis Chamberlain Howell
—Cay Christopher

Little, Brown Books for Young Readers

Hachette Book Group
237 Park Avenue, New York, NY 10017
Visit our Web site at www.lb-kids.com

www.mattchristopher.com

Little, Brown Books for Young Readers is a division of Hachette Book Group, Inc.
The Little, Brown name and logo are trademarks of Hachette Book Group, Inc.

First Paperback Edition: August 2004

Library of Congress Cataloging-in-Publication Data

Hirschfeld, Robert.
    Slam Dunk / text by Robert Hirschfeld.—1st ed.
    p.   cm.
    Summary: When a new school year starts, and thirteen-year-old basketball star Julian feels a lot of pressure as he realizes he is the only remaining player from last year's winning team, a friend's health crisis helps him regain perspective.
    ISBN 978-0-316-60762-9
    [1. Basketball — Fiction.   2. Interpersonal relations — Fiction.
3. Friendship — Fiction.   4. Self perceotion — Fiction.
5. Sick — Fiction.]   I. Title.
PZ7.H59794S1 2004
    [Fic] — dc22

                                                          2003052094

10 9 8 7 6 5

COM-MO

Printed in the United States of America

SLAM DUNK

What's wrong with this picture?

When Julian Pryce was little, he loved the drawings in kids' magazines with that caption. You'd look at the pictures, and everything would seem normal at first, until you noticed that someone in the picture was floating in the air with his feet off the ground, or wearing one black shoe and one white shoe, or that, though it was daytime, a crescent moon hung in the sky. Maybe there would be a dog in a necktie. Something wouldn't make sense.

He felt as if he were staring at one of those drawings now. At first glance, the gym looked pretty much like any gym does when a basketball team is getting ready to work out. There were kids scattered here and there, dribbling, shooting jumpers or foul shots, passing basketballs back and forth, stretching, and goofing around. It all seemed just as it should be.

Julian recognized all the sounds, too. Basketballs thumped the floor and swished through nets. Rubber soles of basketball shoes squeaked as players darted around the court. Boys chattered and laughed and clapped their hands. All of these noises rang out in the high-ceilinged room, much as they usually did.

Even the smells were right: the scent of gleaming hardwood floors that had been recently waxed, of kids sweating and straining in a warm room. And yet . . .

Then he realized what was different. It was the faces. Julian did not see a single familiar face.

It had only been nine months since Julian's team, the Tornadoes, finished its miracle season. They had gone undefeated for the entire year, almost always winning by a wide margin. Then it had been on to the regional play-offs, and then the state championship. The Tornadoes sailed straight through those contests, too.

Last year, twelve-year-old, six-foot-tall Julian had been the star center of the unbeatable Tornadoes. He led the team — and the league — in scoring and rebounding, and set a record for blocked shots. The newspapers gave the Tornadoes a lot of ink, and Julian's picture became a regular feature in sports sections. His long, bony face, framed by curly brown hair, was drawn by cartoonists in the school and town newspapers. There were even write-ups in two national magazines, and some television coverage. It had been like a dream.

Julian had a couple of thick scrapbooks full of clippings, plus a bunch of trophies, plaques, certificates, and other awards decorating his room. Coaches from a few high schools in the area had even sent his family letters, wondering if Julian might want to transfer into their school district. Julian and his family hadn't considered the offers; they were happy where they were.

And then, suddenly, it was over. The cheering and bright lights were just a memory, and all that was left was the stuff in his scrapbooks and the souvenirs in his room.

Now, Julian was thirteen and two inches taller. He was also stronger and faster. He'd been looking forward to the beginning of what he was sure would be another great season for the Tornadoes — but something was wrong.

None of the guys who'd started on last year's team

was anywhere to be seen. Almost every face was new to him. This wasn't totally unexpected, since two of those starters were now too old for the league. But where were the others? Julian looked at the clock. Practice wasn't due to start for a few minutes yet. Maybe they'd show up. He knew that he ought to warm up a little himself, do some stretches, maybe grab a ball and shoot some jumpers. But he stood there, not wanting to get on the floor.

"Yo! Jools! How you doing, dude?"

Hearing his nickname echo through the room, Julian turned. At last, someone he knew! Grady Coughlin stood by the door to the locker room, a big grin on his face. Seeing an old friend and that smile, Julian felt a whole lot better.

Grady had spent most of last season coming off the bench as a substitute point guard. For a few games, when the starting point guard was hurt, he'd been the starter and done well. Julian and Grady had hung out after practices and games. Though he'd seen Grady at school, they hadn't talked about the team. Now, here he was. His straight hair seemed blonder than ever, as if he'd spent lots of time in the sun that summer. But his broad smile was exactly the same.

The boys exchanged low fives.

"Hey, good to see you, man," said Julian. "I was wondering where everyone was. I mean, I knew Danny and Art wouldn't be back, but where are Barry and Max? They should be here, right?"

Grady's sunny smile faded a little. "I heard that Max's family moved last month. His dad got a job out of state, I think. But Barry, he'll show up. He always used to get here at the last minute. Remember Coach Valenti getting on his case about that?"

Julian wasn't happy to hear about Max, a solid forward who always provided tough defense. "Max moved? That's too bad."

Grady shrugged. "Yeah, I liked Max, too. And he really knew how to cover a guy. Great D. But hey, Barry'll give us some points, and he can clean up on the boards. And don't forget the Tornadoes' secret weapon."

Julian stared at Grady. "Secret weapon?"

Grady nodded. "Right! Me, man! I'll be at point guard this year! I guarantee I'll feed you the ball plenty!"

Julian couldn't help laughing. "Oh, yeah, right. How could I forget?" He felt better, although it would have been cool to have three of the championship starting five back again.

"And the coach'll be here, too," Grady pointed out. "He'll put this team together. He always does."

Julian knew that Grady had a point. Coach Valenti always seemed to come up with winning teams. And Barry Streeter had a deadly jump shot from almost anywhere on the court. He also knew how to box out opponents and position himself for rebounds if Julian couldn't get them. The Tornadoes would be all right.

Grady nudged Julian's arm. "Here's the coach now. You know the dude with him?"

Julian shook his head. "Never saw him before." Coach Valenti had entered the gym from the locker room with a boy in shorts and a sweatshirt with the sleeves cut off. The coach was talking to the boy, who looked around nervously. Julian thought the guy looked like a forward — pretty tall, strong-looking legs, and broad shoulders.

A moment later, the coach reached for the whistle hanging around his neck and blew a couple of short, shrill blasts.

"Everybody, can I have your attention?" he called out. "Group up over here, guys."

The chatter and activity stopped as the boys gathered around the coach and the newcomer.

Coach Valenti looked around at the boys and smiled.

"I see a lot of new faces. Well . . . good! We need new blood because some talented players aren't back this year. That's one reason I enjoy coaching the Tornadoes — there are always changes to be made and adjustments to work out. Before we get started, I have some news to pass along."

Grady whispered so that only Julian could hear him. "I guess Barry's still having trouble making it on time, huh?"

Julian nodded and smiled, never taking his eyes off the coach and the boy with him.

The coach continued. "We'll say hello to each other shortly. In two weeks, we play our first game, and you'll know each other well by then. Let me introduce a player whose family is new in town. This is Mick Reiss. Mick was a forward with his old team, and he'll be a forward with the Tornadoes, too."

Mick muttered a quiet "Hi," and several boys waved and mumbled greetings back.

"There's another piece of news I have to report, news that isn't very good at all," said Coach Valenti, his face serious. "I learned this morning that Barry Streeter, who some of you remember as an outstanding forward last season, was hurt in a car accident last night. It's not known yet how serious his injuries are. But we do know that Barry can't be here today and that he'll be lost to the Tornadoes for some time."

There was stirring and some whispers among the players. Julian stared at Coach Valenti in shock. His first thought was of Barry lying hurt in a hospital. But something else was bothering him, too. All of last year's starting team was *gone!*

Except for *him.*

The coach quieted everyone. "Of course, I see a few guys here who I know will be able to get us moving in the right direction. Plus, I'm sure that some of you other boys will make contributions, too. But the fact is that we have a challenge facing us and just two weeks to make ourselves into a team. I'm sure we can do it if we put our minds and bodies into it."

The coach went on talking about what players would have to do, how hard work would pay off, and how the result could be a fine team, and so on and so forth. But Julian wasn't listening. He tuned the coach out and looked around the gym at the other boys.

This was bad news. *Very* bad news.

It had come on so fast that he was only now realizing how bad it was. At first, he'd figured it would be up to Max, Barry, and him. Well . . . and Grady. Then he found out it was just Barry and him. Now it was all on Julian's shoulders. All on *him*.

Suddenly, he remembered the hard work he'd put in last season: the warm-ups and drills, the scrimmages and sweating and aches and hassles. Last year, it led to a dream season, an undefeated team, a state championship.

But this year, he'd have to work just as hard, and the result might be . . . no, *had to be* . . . worse. Maybe a lot worse.

He heard Coach Valenti say "I'm glad to see that our all-star center, Julian Pryce, is back and looking good. He was a big part of our success last year, and he'll be a big part of our success this year as well."

Everyone turned to stare at Julian. Most of them smiled. He tried to smile back, but his mind was still reeling. Last year, he'd been a hero on an unstoppable team. What would happen if . . . no, make that *when* . . . they lost? Who would get the blame? Whose fault would it be? Whom would the newspapers and the crowds point to?

They'd point to *him*. They'd blame *him*.

It wasn't fair.

Coach Valenti began practice with some stretching, followed by warm-up drills. Julian, who had been looking forward to getting the new season started, suddenly found himself unable to work up any energy or enthusiasm. After loafing his way through the stretches, he took it easy as the drills began, concentrating on watching the other players and deciding whether he saw any talent there.

The team split into two lines for a layup drill. The first player in the right-hand line took the ball to the basket and laid it in, then went to the end of the left-hand line. The first player in that line grabbed the ball and passed to the next player from the right line before running to the end of the line on the right, and so on. After a while, the coach had the players from the left-hand line shoot, while the ones in the right line grabbed the rebounds.

Julian took the ball on his first feed and made an easy, effortless layup. He was confident he could make those shots all day long. He focused on the other guys. Grady showed a lot of hustle, as he always had, and was a good passer; no news there. The new guy, Mick, looked nervous. He could jump, but he fumbled the ball when it was passed to him. *Bad hands,* Julian decided. Another new guy, whose name Julian didn't remember, looked as though he might have good hands, but he didn't get off the floor very well. This one had red hair and freckles. As for the others, Julian didn't see anyone do anything worth noticing.

After the layup drill, they ran a dribbling relay, with the team divided in half and players dribbling the full length of the court and back, passing off to the next guy in line until both squads had finished. Here, Grady was at his best. The guy really could dribble and cover ground quickly. One or two other newbies were okay, but several looked as if they had never seen a basketball, much less dribbled one. Mick wasn't too hot at putting the ball to the floor, Julian noted. Of course, he wasn't one to talk. Dribbling had always been his own major weakness.

"Too much arm movement, Mick!" called the coach as Mick dribbled downcourt. "Use more wrist and less elbow . . . that's better! And try keeping the ball lower so it's easier to maneuver."

When Julian's turn came, the coach called out, "Julian, you got weights around your ankles? Let's see a little more hustle!"

Julian felt annoyed and singled out. He didn't really try to pick it up. After all, it was just the first day.

A little later, Coach Valenti worked on one of basketball's most basic and classic plays, the pick-and-roll. In the pick-and-roll, one offensive player creates a stationary block, or pick, on a defender. Another offensive player moves as if he's about to shoot. Instead, he feeds the ball to the pick, who is pivoting, or rolling, toward the hoop. When done right, the pick-and-roll results in an easy layup. The play had been a Tornado specialty the previous year.

In the pick-and-roll drill, two offensive players were matched against two on defense. Julian and Grady worked as an offensive pairing, as they had sometimes done in the past. Grady dribbled toward where Julian had set his pick. But Julian was slow making his roll, and Grady's pass sailed past him and out-of-bounds. Julian shook his head and trotted after the ball. As he came back with it, he noticed that Coach Valenti was looking at him, clearly not pleased by what he'd seen. But the coach didn't say anything. Grady, too, gave Julian a puzzled look.

Julian watched other players run the same drill and decided that they looked pretty lame. So far, it seemed that his worst fears were proving to be accurate. Meanwhile, Grady kept up a stream of chatter designed to cheer on the rest of the guys. A few other players were also clapping their hands and shouting encouragement. Julian thought it sounded silly.

After a few more drills, the coach called for a break. Grady approached Julian. "You all right?" he asked.

Julian stared at the other boy. "Huh? Sure. Why?"

Grady shrugged. "I don't know, it's just . . . I thought maybe something was wrong, like maybe you don't feel well."

"I'm fine," insisted Julian.

Grady saw Mick Reiss standing nearby, looking hesitant about approaching, and smiled. "Yo, Mick! Looking good out there!"

"Well, thanks," Mick said quietly. "I felt kind of rusty, but I'll work it out, I guess. Uh . . . Julian? Hi, I'm Mick."

Julian nodded toward the new guy. "Hi."

Mick stood silently for a moment, as if waiting for Julian to say more. But Julian said nothing. Finally, Mick blurted, "I'm really looking forward to playing with you. I saw the state semis last year, when you scored twenty-six and pulled down twelve boards. It was awesome."

Julian gave Mick a very thin smile. "Thanks."

Grady glanced at Julian and then faced Mick. "You have a good shooting touch yourself, man. I bet you see a lot of playing time this year, right, Jools?"

Julian said, "Yeah, well. Barry's out, so . . . I guess." He kneeled down and retied a shoelace.

Grady said, "Good to have you here, Mick."

Out of the corner of his eye, Julian saw Mick walk away. He stood up to find Grady staring at him with narrowed eyes.

After a moment, Julian said, "*What?*"

Grady sighed and muttered, "Nothing, man. Not a thing."

When practice resumed, Julian told himself to get it

into high gear but somehow couldn't do it. The coach did a one-on-one drill in which a defender tried to get the ball away from an offensive player, who had to keep dribbling until the coach stopped play. If the player stopped dribbling — "picked up the dribble" — it was the same as if the defender had taken the ball away, because the offensive player was trapped and couldn't start dribbling again.

Julian went head-to-head against the red-haired newbie, who introduced himself as Len. Julian started to dribble, but Len had quick hands and swiped the ball away almost immediately. On his second try, Julian held on to the ball a little longer. Len reached in to flick it away for the second time. Julian, without thinking, clutched the ball in both hands, meaning that he'd picked up his dribble. Julian winced as Coach Valenti blew his whistle.

"Switch to defense, Julian," said the coach. "Maybe you can get it back."

But Len shielded the ball with his body, and when Julian tried to reach around him, Len whirled past him toward the basket and took an easy layup. When Len took the ball from the coach for a second time, Julian gave the other boy more room, staying a few feet away. Len didn't try to get around Julian, but Julian didn't come close to getting the ball, either. Finally, Julian leaned forward, blocked Len with his body, and snatched at the ball, but the coach whistled play to a halt.

"That's a blocking foul," he said to Julian. "You were all over him. Come on, you know better than that. On defense, you have to use your *feet*."

Julian's face turned hot, and he knew that he was blushing. He wasn't used to being talked to like that by Coach Valenti. He felt humiliated, and he resented Len for showing him up.

"Okay, let's have two more guys out there," said the coach. Julian moved stiffly to the sidelines and glared out at the court.

How come the coach got on my case like that? he wondered. *This isn't a game. It isn't even an important practice session. It's the first day, that's all!*

Okay, Julian admitted to himself, *I didn't hustle. But Coach Valenti knows I'll be there when it's crunch time!*

In this angry frame of mind, Julian watched the rest of the team go through the drill. He wasn't impressed by what he saw. This bunch wasn't anywhere near as good as the Tornadoes of last season. He was going to have to carry them on his back, and they would probably lose anyway.

And what was the deal with Grady? The point guard kept on talking it up, clapping his hands, being a cheerleader. What for? Julian found his mood getting worse and worse. As practice continued, Julian's performance became less and less energetic.

When the session ended, the coach spoke to the team, sounding surprisingly cheerful and optimistic. Julian was startled at first but decided that the coach had to give the impression that everything was going well, even when it clearly wasn't.

"Okay," Coach Valenti said, "I think we have the makings of a solid team here. See you all tomorrow, same time, same place."

As the Tornadoes headed for the locker room, Julian hung back, unwilling to join in the talking and joking of his teammates. Grady came over to him.

"Listen, a few guys are going to get something to eat and hang out. Want to come?"

Julian shook his head. "I better not. I have a lot to do at home. See you tomorrow."

"You sure?" Grady asked. "Come on, just for a little while."

"I told you," replied Julian, trying not to sound grumpy, "I can't today."

Grady nodded. "Listen, maybe I'll give you a call later, all right?"

"Yeah, sure," Julian said, hoping nobody else would try to talk to him. He just didn't feel like it.

He changed clothes in the locker room and slowly walked home alone. What had happened in the last few hours? He'd arrived at the gym really pumped, ready to get working, eager for what he was sure would be a good season. Now everything was ruined. The team was going to be no better than ordinary, and maybe worse. Most of his teammates were strangers, and he wasn't looking forward to spending a lot of time with them, or to going through a lot of tiring, boring workouts. Was there anything he could do to make it better?

At the moment, it didn't seem as if there was.

3

Earth to Julian. Come in, Julian. Can you hear me?"

Julian looked up from his dinner plate to see his older sister, Megan, grinning at him. Megan played soccer on her high school team. Though not a gifted athlete, she was a tough competitor who loved the sport and gave everything she had whenever she played.

Now she looked more closely at her brother and asked, "Seriously, what's up, bro? You really look down. You feeling all right?"

Julian recalled Grady asking him the same question during practice. "I'm *fine*," he snapped.

"Whoa!" said Megan, shielding her face with her arms in mock terror. "Okay, you're fine. I'm glad to hear it."

Julian's father, who was helping himself to a second

slab of meat loaf, said, "You do look down, champ. Is anything on your mind?"

"Wasn't this the first day of basketball practice?" asked his mother. "Did it go well?"

Julian sighed and shoved away his plate. "It didn't go too great. This year's team is . . ." He shook his head.

"What's wrong?" asked Mr. Pryce.

Julian explained that Barry was injured and that all the other starters from last year were gone.

"And the new guys look really lame," he said. "We're going to be bad this year, and I'll be the guy who gets all the grief because I'm this big star. It's a lousy deal."

"Hold on," said Megan. "Today was your first practice? So this was the first time you saw most of the guys play?"

Julian nodded.

Megan hooted. "You say the team stinks after *one practice?* Lighten up a little; give it time! It's way too early to give up."

"I didn't say I was giving up!" Julian retorted. "All I said was —"

"Settle down," said Mr. Pryce. "There's no need to

raise your voice like that. And Megan has a point. Give Coach Valenti some time and some credit."

"Anyway," Megan went on, "what if it turns out that you're right, and the team isn't all that good? What if you lose some games? Are you saying you don't want to play unless you're sure you can win everything?"

"I didn't say that," Julian muttered.

His mother said, "After what you boys did last season, this year is almost sure to be less successful, isn't it?"

"Maybe it makes sense to wait awhile before deciding how good the Tornadoes are," Mr. Pryce said as he cut into his meat loaf.

"Yeah, cheer up, bro," suggested Megan. "It probably isn't all that bad."

Julian had hoped for more sympathy from his family, more understanding, but it sounded as if they weren't going to offer it. As soon as he could do so, he left the table and went to his room. He spent a moment looking at the trophies, framed pictures and clippings, and other souvenirs from last season. It didn't look as though he'd be adding much to the collection this year. He flopped onto his bed, thinking it would be nice to find *somebody* who understood what he was going through.

21

When the phone rang, he let someone downstairs answer it. Then he heard his father's voice call out.

"Julian! Phone call! It's Grady."

Julian groaned to himself. He was not in a good mood, and the idea of talking to Grady didn't appeal to him at all. But he also knew that if he didn't speak to Grady, his parents would want to know why, and that seemed even less appealing. He picked up the phone.

"Hi."

"Hey, Jools, what's up?" Even through a phone line, Grady sounded cheerful and full of energy. Julian frowned.

"Not much," he replied. "What's up with you?"

"Oh, nothing," Grady said. "Hey, a bunch of us went over to the ice cream shop this afternoon. Mick was there, and this guy Len Hornsby, and a few other guys — I don't even know their names yet. I wish you'd have come, too."

"Well, I couldn't make it. Like I said," Julian replied, lying on his back with the phone tucked under his chin.

"Yeah, right. Anyway . . ." Grady paused. It was as though he wasn't exactly sure what he wanted to say next. After a few seconds, he went on.

"They're really all right," he said. "Mick is a cool

guy, and Len is sort of quiet but I think he's pretty nice, too. And they *all* kept talking about how great a player you are. I mean, they really look up to you."

Julian wondered if Grady was exaggerating, trying to persuade Julian to be nicer to the new players. As he listened to Grady chatter on, he looked up at a framed picture on the wall — it was of him, with Barry on one side and Max on the other. The three of them were grinning like idiots at the camera and had their arms draped over one another's shoulders. Julian knew he would miss them, on and off the court.

He realized that Grady had stopped talking and was waiting for him to say something back. "Uh, well . . . I'm glad you had a good time," he said.

"Well, we really did," said Grady. "And I think when you get to know them, you'll like them, too. I mean, sure, it won't be like last year, but we're going to have a good team. I think we could make the play-offs."

Julian couldn't help chuckling. "Yeah, huh? Well, it's good you feel that way," he said, not wanting to give his own opinion of the team. But Grady sensed what Julian was thinking.

"Yeah," said Grady after a moment, "I *do* feel that way. And I'm sorry you don't."

Even though Grady wasn't doing anything but speaking the truth, Julian was annoyed.

"How do you know what I feel? Did you learn how to read minds or something?"

"Oh, come on, Julian," Grady said. "You don't have to say a word. It's obvious what you think about this team. You think we're pretty bad. And it's not fair, because —"

"First of all," Julian said, cutting Grady off, "you can't say what I'm thinking unless I tell you. And second, I can think anything I want."

"You don't know how good the Tornadoes are yet," insisted Grady. "Nobody does. It's too soon to know. And I think we're going to be pretty tough — partly because you're the center, and partly because we have some other guys who can play hard, too. But it doesn't help the team if you treat those new guys the way you did today. You're the —"

"What did I do?" Julian demanded. "Did I insult them? I didn't do anything!"

"Right!" replied Grady. "You didn't do *anything*. You hardly talked to them, you didn't make them feel welcome, you didn't have a nice word to say to them. That's *real* helpful."

"It's not my job to be a cheerleader," Julian said.

"You're the main man," Grady snapped. "Mick came up and wanted to talk, but what did you do? You acted like he wasn't even there! You couldn't be bothered to make him feel like part of the team, and don't tell me that's not part of your job, because it *is*."

Julian sat up straight on the edge of his bed. "Wrong. *My job* is to score and rebound and play defense. In *games*. And I'll do that, don't worry."

"You're supposed to set an example," said Grady. "You're the guy everyone looks up to, and that means you can't just score a lot of points and ignore us the rest of the time. Don't you get it? You're the team leader!"

"Nobody asked me to be the team leader!" Julian suddenly realized that he was yelling and that everyone in the house could probably hear him, even with the door closed. He forced himself to speak more quietly.

"Listen, I'll be there for practice, and I'll do what I can to see that the team doesn't look bad. But if you think I'm going to clap my hands and talk about how good everyone's playing when I know they're not, well, too bad. Because that isn't going to happen."

There was silence for a few seconds from Grady's end. Finally, the other boy said, "Man, I don't know what happened to you, but if that's the way you want it, then all right."

"Nothing happened to me. And that's just how I want it."

"Right," Grady said, all the good cheer gone from his voice. "See you around."

He hung up before Julian had the chance to say good-bye.

As Julian slowly hung up his own phone, there was a knock on his door. Mr. Pryce stuck his head in. "Hi. Everything okay? I thought I heard shouting."

Julian managed a grin. "Everything's fine."

"Well, all right then," said his father. "Sorry to bother you, but I thought, maybe . . . I guess I didn't hear right. Take it easy." He closed the door again, leaving Julian alone.

Julian flopped on his bed, wondering what it would be like to be on a team that lost most of the time. He'd never played on a team like that. Maybe he'd have to get used to it. It wasn't a nice thought.

Julian had trouble getting to sleep that night. When he finally did, he had an ugly dream in which he found himself playing basketball and doing everything wrong: missing easy shots, playing terrible defense, making dumb fouls, all in front of a huge crowd of people who kept laughing and jeering at him. He wanted to tell them that he was doing his best, but he couldn't make himself talk. It seemed to go on and on, forever.

When he woke up the following morning, he felt as if he hadn't got any sleep at all.

4

At school the next day, Julian thought about Grady and their angry phone conversation. He knew he had been out of line. A lot of what he'd said had been said just because he was feeling bad. When he spotted Grady in a crowded hallway between classes, he hurried over to talk to him.

"Hey, wait up! I'm sorry about last night. I was a jerk. I didn't mean what I said."

Grady nodded, and then he smiled. "I felt bad last night, too. Listen, forget it. It's no big deal. We're still friends, right? That's the main thing."

Julian felt as if a big weight had been taken off his shoulders. "Sure we're still friends! Absolutely! Hey, you want to get together for lunch today?"

"Sounds good," replied Grady. "I'll look for you in the cafeteria, okay?"

"Cool," said Julian. The boys touched fists, then hurried off to their classes.

The cafeteria was noisy and crowded when Julian arrived. He felt a tap on his shoulder from behind and turned to find Grady standing there.

"What a zoo, huh?" said Grady.

"Absolutely," Julian agreed, looking around for a place to sit.

Grady pointed across the room. "Hey, there's Mick. Come on, there are empty chairs across from him." Grady started across the room, leaving Julian to catch up. Julian followed, but not eagerly. He'd been looking forward to spending a half hour with Grady, just the two of them. But there was no graceful way to get out of this situation, so he decided he'd have to make the best of it.

Mick had looked lonely, but he brightened up when he caught sight of Grady and Julian approaching. "Hey! You joining me?"

"Definitely!" Grady said, sliding into a plastic chair across from Mick. He pointed to Mick's cafeteria tray and made a face. "You actually get your lunch *here?* You're a brave man."

Julian sat down next to Grady.

"Actually," Mick said, "this isn't so bad. You should've seen what they sold at my old school. Makes this stuff look pretty good."

Grady made a face. "Get outa here! It was worse than the mystery meat they serve here? No way!"

Julian unwrapped his lunch. He nudged Grady and asked, "Think Max is playing ball where he's living now?"

"Was Max a guy from last year's team?" Mick asked.

Grady nodded. "Yeah. Good player and a nice guy."

Mick whistled. "That was some team. I only saw you guys that one time, but you looked pretty awesome."

"We'll be good this year, too," Grady said. "Coach Valenti is excellent. You'll see."

Mick waved to someone behind Julian and called out, "Yo! Len! Over here!" He pointed to an empty chair next to his.

Redheaded Len Hornsby sat down and nodded to Julian and Grady. Julian's mood was turning bad. He'd hoped to hang with Grady, but these strangers kept butting in.

Mick turned to Len. "I was just saying, I saw the Tornadoes play last year. They were tough!" He looked at Julian. "What was it like having all the reporters and TV cameras around like that? Was it fun?"

Julian shrugged. "Was it fun? I don't know, sometimes maybe, I guess."

"It was unbelievable!" Grady said. "I mean, we never expected to go all the way to the state title. Sometimes it was scary, but sure, it was fun, too. We got to meet a lot of stars. Jools, remember when we talked to those NBA guys at that dinner? That was fun!"

"NBA? As in the *National Basketball Association*?" Len's eyes were wide.

"Yeah, at the awards dinner," Grady said. "And Jools got his Most Valuable Player trophy from the governor! The governor said that the state was proud of us, and that he looked forward to reading about us doing great things."

"Really?" Mick asked. "You have pictures of yourself with the governor?"

"Uh-huh," Julian muttered.

"We all got a shot of the governor standing with the team," Grady said. "He seemed like a nice guy. And we were in the audience of a few TV shows and got to be special guests at some college games."

"Amazing," Mick said.

31

"You better believe it!" Grady said. "We used to laugh about it and wonder when we were going to wake up."

Julian laughed. "Funny thing . . . *we* did this and *we* did that . . . pretty funny. All that *we* and *us*."

"Huh?" Grady looked puzzled. "What do you mean? It's all true, right?"

"Sure," Julian said. "It's all true. It all happened, all that stuff. It's just funny, all this *we* stuff from a guy who mostly sat on the bench last year."

Mick and Len exchanged a quick look and then focused on their food.

Grady narrowed his eyes. "I remember that I was in those pictures, too. I played in some of the games and was there, working hard, at every practice. Or was that some kind of dream?"

Julian shrugged. "Oh, I know. You played some."

"I played plenty!" Grady was angry now.

Mick tapped Len's arm. "Let's take off," he said quietly. He and Len stood up and grabbed their stuff.

Grady jerked his chair back and got up. "Hang on. I'm coming, too. I'd rather hang with you guys, if you don't mind. I don't want to bother the big star anymore. Come on."

Julian was now sitting by himself. His appetite vanished. He threw his lunch in a nearby wastebasket. He wandered outside and sat on a bench in front of the school.

I shouldn't have got on Grady's case like that. Grady had been part of the team, even if he wasn't a starter.

That was the key, Julian suddenly realized. Grady hadn't been a starter. He didn't know what it was like to lead the team to victory time and again — or to feel the pressure to stay on top, knowing that even one loss, one sloppy game, would ruin a perfect record. Last year, Julian had shared that pressure with four other starters, guys like Barry and Max, whose skills and talent matched his own and who had helped make Julian a star . . . *the* star.

But now he was the sole remaining starter. Now it was Julian and a bunch of question marks, many of whose names he didn't even know yet. Without Barry and Max and the others, he wouldn't look as good, and that bothered him.

Grady said that Julian had to be *the* leader, *the* example, for everybody else. Not *a* leader, *an* example. It was up to him. Well, he didn't want to be that guy. He hadn't asked to be put in that position. That scared him.

All the work and effort that had gone into making last year's team what it was — he'd have to do all that work again. The same workouts, the same drilling and running and sweating . . . the whole deal. The difference was that at the end of the year, there would be a lot less to show for it. There had to be. And that discouraged him.

None of this was Grady's fault, or Mick's or Len's or anybody's. Julian knew that, but he couldn't help how he felt — *trapped*.

5

That afternoon, for the first time ever, Julian was late to practice. When he arrived, the rest of the team was already in the gym warming up. He changed into his workout gear as quickly as he could and walked out on the court to see the players running the usual layup drill. The coach saw him and came over.

"Hi. How come you're late?"

For a moment, Julian thought about coming up with some kind of excuse but gave up the notion almost immediately. He didn't want to be a liar in addition to showing up late. But he didn't want to tell the truth either — that he simply didn't want to walk into the locker room and face Grady. He couldn't say that.

So he said, "Sorry. No excuse. I won't be late again."

"Uh-huh," said the coach, fixing Julian with a stony stare. "Just so we understand each other completely, nobody on this team is allowed to break my rules. And showing up on time is one of the most important ones. I'll take your word that it won't happen again. Take some laps around the gym until I tell you to join the rest of the team."

Julian nodded and began jogging around the floor, watching the drill as he went. It was the usual stuff, and it looked . . . well . . . dumb. The guys went in for uncontested layups, something that rarely happened in a game. When it did happen, it led to an automatic two points.

But his teammates were missing too many layups. Passes were poorly thrown. Instead of smoothly laying the ball in, the pass receiver had to break stride, sometimes even chase a ball that got away completely. And through it all, Grady was telling the guys how good they looked, even when they didn't.

A few minutes later, Coach Valenti signaled for Julian to join the team. When his turn came to try for a layup, Julian took the ball and went as high as he could before letting it bounce off the glass and through the hoop. As he trotted to the end of the other line, Julian heard several of the players clapping and whispering to one another. He knew he'd made an impressive-looking shot.

A moment later, he soared equally high to pull down a rebound after a missed layup and tossed a perfect pass to the next man in line. That player was able to shoot without even a slight adjustment in stride. If Grady had said anything complimentary about Julian's moves, Julian hadn't heard it. And Coach Valenti's face remained expressionless. But Julian knew he'd looked good. He felt a sudden surge of energy, a sense of re-discovering how talented he was.

The coach called the team together. "Some of you remember the sidestep drill from last year . . . and you probably hated it. But you need it to play tough D. First, make two lines down the middle of the court from one basket to the other. Make sure there's some room between you and your neighbor . . . good. Now, face the other line."

Julian found himself staring at Mick. The two boys nodded to each other.

"You don't play good defense with your hands," Coach Valenti said. "You play good D with your *feet*. When you play man-to-man, you have to stay right on the guy you're guarding, keep him out of scoring lanes, and that means moving from side to side. When I blow the whistle, you'll keep your hands up, like *this*" — he stretched out his arms with his hands just under shoulder height — "and you'll move sideways, in this direction" — he gestured to Julian's left — "until I blow the whistle again. Then you'll move to the other side and switch again when I blow the whistle, and so on.

"Remember, keep your arms up and be alert, because sometimes I'll blow that whistle pretty fast. Don't slow down; don't let me see anyone loafing. Ready?"

The whistle blew, and Julian moved to his left, his arms high. Before very long, his spurt of energy was gone, and he was breathing hard. He wanted to slow down, but Mick was managing to keep up the pace, forcing him to do likewise. His arms started to feel heavy.

Sometimes the coach blew the whistle only a second after the last blast, and the players would reverse direction after only a step or two.

"Watch those hands!" Coach Valenti called out. "Keep 'em up! Len, don't slow down. Come on, guys, it'll get easier in a week or two. Julian, don't drag those feet!"

After what felt like hours but was only a few minutes, the coach said, "All right! Take a break. We'll run this drill every day because you need the work."

Julian bent over, his hands on his knees, and tried to catch his breath. Mick was gasping, too, and caught Julian's eye. He smiled and said, "Man! He's pretty tough!"

Julian nodded, took a deep breath, and said, "Believe it." He thought about doing this every day, probably for a little longer each time, and stifled a groan.

"Well, it's a good workout," said Mick. "Wish we'd done this with my old team."

Julian walked over to grab a towel from a courtside bench and mopped his face. As he did, he heard Grady's voice. "Mind if I talk?"

Julian put down the towel and said, "I shouldn't have said that stuff about you being a sub. That wasn't fair."

Grady shrugged. "You're right, it wasn't fair."

"That's what I said," Julian replied, a resentful edge in his voice.

"I wish you'd lighten up with the new guys," Grady said. "You don't have to be their best buddy, just treat them like teammates, which they are."

"Okay," muttered Julian, "I'll do that."

"Because it matters to them, you know?" Grady went on, as if Julian hadn't said anything.

Julian gave Grady a long look. "I said I would, all right?"

"Sure," Grady said, turning away. "Sorry I bothered you."

When the break was over, the coach worked on set plays, including the give-and-go. In this play, a tall offensive player, a center or a forward, posts himself with his back to the basket near the key and gets the ball from a teammate. He then passes off and pivots around the man guarding him toward the hoop. The player with the ball feeds the tall man, who, if the play is run correctly, should have an open layup.

Julian was the man in the middle the first time it was run, and he was guarded by Mick. He passed to Grady and moved around Mick to the basket. Grady's pass was right on target, setting up an easy shot.

"Very nice!" called out Coach Valenti. Julian smiled and nodded to Grady, who smiled back. Julian had to admit that nothing felt better than working a play like that properly.

A few minutes later, Julian was in the pivot again, and this time Len was the guy he passed to. Julian made his move around the guy guarding him, but his first step was slow. When Len launched his pass, Julian wasn't in position to get it. Shaking his head, Julian slowly trotted after the ball.

"Get the lead out," the coach called. "The pass was where it should have been, Julian."

Julian kept his face neutral, but inside he was seething. Like nobody else had messed up a play today?

Coach Valenti spent the last part of practice working on zone defense. In this type of defense, defenders don't guard individuals but are responsible for guarding a section of the court. Julian was the center on the offensive team, and he was feeling tired and moving as little as possible. The defensive team was using a 3–2 zone, with a defender on each side of the key. Julian's responsibility was to work himself open for a possible shot, but he stayed pretty much in one place.

Finally, there was a blast from the coach's whistle. "Julian, you know about the three-second rule, don't you?"

The three-second rule says that no player from the offensive team can stand with even one foot in the key for more than three seconds. If someone does, the team has to turn the ball over. Julian knew the rule very well. He nodded, feeling foolish.

41

Coach Valenti said, "Well, you've had your right foot planted in the paint for about ten seconds now. You stuck on a piece of chewing gum or something?"

"Uh . . . sorry." Julian realized that the coach was absolutely right and moved away.

"Okay, let's knock off for today," said the coach. "We did some good work out there. Before everyone leaves, I have some news. Barry Streeter's dad called me to say that Barry is going to need surgery on his leg. He'll be in the hospital for a few days, and it isn't clear yet how long it'll take him to recover.

"Needless to say, this is bad news, and Barry could use some cheering up and a show of support. Visiting hours are until eight P.M., so please, everyone, stop by if you possibly can. Okay, that's it. Julian, stick around a minute."

As the rest of the players left the floor, Julian braced himself for a lecture. The coach motioned him to sit down on one of the courtside benches.

"What's up?" asked Coach Valenti. His voice was mild. "I don't want to poke my nose into anything that isn't my business, but something's bothering you, and if you want to talk about it, feel free."

Julian was relieved that the coach wasn't yelling.

"I'm okay," he said, feeling as if he'd repeated those words a million times recently.

The coach thought a moment before saying, "Last year, it wasn't just your skills that set you apart. It was your attitude. You were always early for practices and games, and you gave it all you had. If I worried about anything, it was that you might push yourself too hard.

"That was then. This year, you show up late to our second practice, with no excuse at all. You don't seem to want to have anything to do with your teammates, and you're going at about half-speed. I know it's early, but the difference is huge, and I'm . . . concerned. Not angry, not worried, but definitely concerned. But you say you're okay, so I'll accept that. *But* I need to see more from you than I've seen so far.

"It's partly because the team needs the kind of play you're capable of, and it's partly because we have so many new faces. That puts more of a burden on you than there would have been if more of last year's guys were back. Like it or not, you're the one who sets the tone. If you slack off, I guarantee others will. And then we're in for a long season."

"So if the team doesn't do well, it's my fault?" Julian asked.

The coach shook his head. "What I said was, you have to show the way: make this team think and play together, and give an effort. It may not be fair, but that's what happens when someone has a gift. *You* have a gift. Basketball may take you a long way, but there will be a price to pay. Think about it. And remember, I'll always be around if you want to talk." He stood up to leave. "See you tomorrow," Coach Valenti said. "On time."

Julian headed for the locker room, thinking about what the coach had said. As he changed clothes, Grady came over. "Hey, my mom is driving Mick and me to visit Barry in the hospital, if you feel like coming. We're leaving in a few minutes."

Without really thinking, Julian said, "I can't. I have to go home."

"You don't want to see Barry?" asked Grady. "The coach said —"

"*Sure* I want to see him!" Julian glared at the other boy. "But I can't go this afternoon, that's all. I have to go home."

"Okay then." Grady walked away without another word. Julian put on his street shoes, wondering if he had done the right thing. He was worried about Barry and did want to see him. Why had he turned Grady down?

Because he wanted to see Barry without anybody else along.

But that was *dumb*. He should have agreed and gone with the others. Why was he behaving this way? He looked around. He was the only player still there.

Suddenly, Julian jumped up, grabbed his gear, and raced outside. Maybe he could still catch Grady and Mick.

But when he got outside, they were gone.

6

For the rest of the day, Julian kept thinking about not going to visit Barry with Grady. When he sat down to dinner, he told his family about Barry's condition.

"Could you guys drive me over to the hospital after dinner so I can see him?"

"Sure thing," said Mr. Pryce. "I know Barry would appreciate it. I'll run you over there. As long as I'm taking you, is there anyone else who might like to go along? How about your friend Grady?"

Julian said, "No, that's okay. Just me."

"Why don't you give Grady a call and tell him you're going?" Mrs. Pryce persisted. "After all, he's one of Barry's friends, too."

Julian realized he would have to explain. "Grady, uh . . . he already went to see Barry. He went right after practice."

"Oh," said Julian's mother, looking a little surprised and glancing at her husband.

"How come you didn't go with Grady?" Megan asked. "Didn't he ask you to go?"

"Yeah," Julian said, wishing the conversation would end. "He asked."

"Well?" Megan said. "If Grady went this afternoon, *and* he asked you to come along . . . why didn't you?"

Julian stared straight ahead. "Because he . . . I didn't . . . we kind of had a fight."

Mr. Pryce frowned. "You and Grady? What's going on? You two always got along last season."

Julian didn't want to go into it. "It's no big deal. It's just . . ."

"You don't have to talk about it if you don't want to," said his mother.

"I think it's weird that you wouldn't visit your buddy in the hospital together," Megan said, looking at Julian disapprovingly. "Especially if it's no big deal."

Julian felt his face turning red. "He was hassling me, that's all. Telling me how I should act with the new guys on the team, saying that I'm not doing what I'm supposed to be doing, like I'm goofing off, not giving a hundred percent. And I got angry."

47

"The way you talked about how bad the team was," Megan said, "maybe he's right."

"Mind your own business!" Julian yelled. "He was wrong, and so are you!"

Mr. Pryce held up a hand like a policeman directing traffic. "That's enough of that, both of you. Megan, it really isn't your business, unless Julian asks you for advice."

"I'd like to see Grady and you patch things up," said Julian's mother. "It's never fun to have problems with a friend."

"Well, he started it," muttered Julian.

"Doesn't matter who started it," said Mr. Pryce. "The main thing is that it's bad for both of you, and it could be bad for the team as well. Anyway, I'll take you to the hospital."

A little later, Julian sat in the family car with his father. Mr. Pryce asked, "Were you and Grady arguing last night on the phone?"

"Uh-huh," Julian admitted.

They pulled into the hospital parking lot. "Want me to come?" asked Mr. Pryce.

"That's okay," said Julian. "I'll call you when I'm ready to leave, okay?"

48

He went in and was directed to Barry's room. Feeling nervous, he approached the open door, not knowing what to expect, and peered in.

"Hello?" he said, entering the room.

"Jools! My man!" Barry looked surprised and happy to see him.

Julian was shocked by his friend's appearance and hoped it didn't show. Barry's right leg was encased in a cast from his foot almost to his hip. A complicated-looking metal frame around the cast kept the leg from moving. His left forearm was heavily bandaged, and there was a large dressing wrapped around his head. Something dripped from a plastic IV bag on a pole into a needle stuck into his right arm, just below the elbow.

Julian hadn't realized that Barry's injuries were so serious. Now he struggled to think of something to say, wanting to sound relaxed rather than worried, looking for a cheerful thought but not finding one.

Barry grinned. "Do I look that bad? You should see the expression on your face."

Julian came to the side of the bed. "Uh . . . I didn't realize . . . I guess you won't be at practice tomorrow."

Laughing, Barry said, "No, but I got a note from my

49

doctor. You just missed my folks; they left a minute ago. Good to see you, man."

Julian pulled over a chair and sat. "What's up? I hear you need an operation. When?"

Barry's smile dimmed. "Probably tomorrow, if the doctors are sure I don't have an infection." With his left hand, he gestured to the IV. "That's why I'm getting the antibiotics, just in case. I won't know until the morning."

"Wow," Julian said. "That's rough. Did the doctors say when you can play again?"

Barry leaned back into his pillows and closed his eyes. "Uh-uh. They won't know until after they operate. But I don't think it's going to be any time soon."

Julian nodded, trying to take it all in. "But, I mean, you *will* be able to play at some point, right?"

Barry opened his eyes and looked at Julian for a moment, his smile completely gone. "They didn't say. They won't say anything much at all. So, the answer is: I don't know when I can play again. Or *if* I can."

Julian was stuck for something to say. The idea of never being able to play hoops again was more than he could deal with.

"Anyway," Barry said gruffly, "let's talk about something else. How's practice going?"

Julian shook his head. "Okay, I guess. It's a little weird because everybody's gone. Just about, anyway. Max moved away."

"Yeah, I know," Barry replied. "By the way, what's going on with you and Grady?"

Julian stiffened. "Why? What did he tell you? Because whatever he said, he —"

"Grady didn't say anything about you and him," Barry cut in. "It's just, when he showed up and you weren't with him, I asked about you, and he kind of took a deep breath and looked sad and said he didn't want to talk about it. What's the deal?"

"It's nothing," Julian said.

Barry raised his eyebrows in a show of disbelief. "Nothing. Right. Except you and he came to see me separately, and he wouldn't say why and you won't talk about it. Hey, I'm your friend, and I'm his friend, so come on. Tell me."

Julian stood up and started to pace around the room. "He's hassling me about how I'm supposed to be a 'team leader,' whatever that means. He says I have to, like, be buddies with everyone and hang out with them and be a cheerleader. And that I'm 'setting a bad example' by not hustling. Well, where does he come off telling me what to do? It's none of his business. He keeps saying the Tornadoes are going to be great, which is just dumb. There's no way that's happening, because everybody's gone except me, so when we look bad, it's all going to be my fault. And I didn't sign up to be the great leader; I just want to play basketball."

Julian sat back down by the bed. "Anyway. That's it."

Barry said, "Wow. That's a lot of nothing. But, you know, even if I was on the team, and Max, too, you *would* be the leader. You were our go-to guy last year, the MVP, the big dog. And that's what you're going to be this year, too. You're a star, dude. That's how it is. You're a star. Being a leader is part of the deal, and you can do it."

Julian scowled. "What if I don't *want* to do it? Don't I have a choice?"

Barry said, "Well, you can walk away and quit the team. Which is something you're not going to do. But I don't think you have any other choice. You're a great basketball player, and guys expect a lot out of you, and not just good stats, either. Tell you what, though, I think you're wrong about people blaming you if the Tornadoes aren't champs this year — no one who knows anything about basketball would blame you. They'll have a problem with you if you don't play as well as you can. But if you play hard, nobody's going to give you grief, even if the team never wins a game. At least, that's what I think."

Julian didn't agree with Barry, but he didn't want to argue. Not with Barry looking the way he did and about to have that operation and possibly never being able to play again. Finally, he said, "Grady's crazy if he thinks we'll be a great team, right? No way that can happen, not with a bunch of new guys who are just okay players."

Barry said, "Why are you so down on the new blood? That guy Mick who came over with Grady seems cool, and Grady thinks he can play. Maybe he's as good as me. Who knows?"

"As good as you?" Julian laughed. "No way. I mean he's not bad, but . . ."

"Jools. Hello? Listen up." Barry held up two fingers. "You've had *two* practices. How did we look last year after two practices? Did it look like we'd go all the way? Did we come on like champs? I don't *think* so. We messed up sometimes, and we needed a lot of practice. But we got better. You'll get better this year, too."

Julian wasn't in the mood to be convinced. "Well . . . I guess. I wish you guys were all back, though. It's . . . it's just not fun. And even if we get better, it's not going to be like last year was, that's for sure."

Barry winced as he shifted his body in the bed. "Yeah, I guess it won't. It's not going to be like last year for me, either. How'd you like to switch places?"

Julian blinked, startled. "Whoa, I didn't mean . . . I don't . . . I wouldn't . . ."

"Forget it. Listen, I'm feeling pretty wiped out," Barry said. "I better get some sleep. But it'd be great if you can come back again. I'll be here for a while."

"Sure," Julian replied. "Count on it. Good luck with the operation tomorrow. I'll see you." He stood up to leave.

Barry's answering smile looked tired. "When you come next time, maybe you can do me a favor."

Julian said, "Whatever you want."

"Okay," said Barry. "Next time, I'd like to see you and Grady come together. All right?"

"Uh, sure, if you want. I'll . . . *we'll* be back to see you as soon as we can," Julian said.

Barry reached out and pushed a button, and the head of his bed lowered with a whir.

54

"Excellent. Take it easy, Jools."

"You too," said Julian. "Hang in there."

"I'll give it my best shot," said Barry, closing his eyes. "Don't worry so much, and everything will be cool."

As Julian reached the door, he looked back. Barry suddenly seemed very tired and not at all happy.

7

The next morning, Julian came into the kitchen to find his sister having breakfast. Megan asked, "How's Barry?"

"Not great," Julian said, sitting across from his sister as he waited for his toast. "His leg had this gigantic metal thing on it, and he was all bandaged up. Plus, he had stuff going into his arm from a plastic bag through a needle. He's probably going to have an operation today, and he doesn't know if he can play ball again."

Megan stared. "You mean, *never*?"

Julian got up for his toast and sat back down. "The doctors won't say. But maybe never. I didn't know what to tell him."

He kept seeing Barry in his memory, looking the way he did in the hospital bed. He felt his eyes blur and looked away so Megan wouldn't see them.

56

"That's terrible, Jools. What could you have said?" Megan's voice was unusually soft. "Look, you went to see him, and you'll see him again. You're doing what a friend is supposed to do. You're there for him, right?"

"Oh, yeah, right," Julian muttered. "All I did was complain about Grady and the team and . . . just me, me, me. Some friend *I* am."

"Don't give yourself such a hard time," said Megan. "Take it easy, all right?"

"Well, I should've tried to cheer him up instead of whining."

Megan put down her juice glass and stared at her brother. "Cheer him up? Yeah, sure, you should have cheered him up. He's going to have this operation, and he doesn't know what shape he'll be in afterward. You really think you could have made him forget his problems? Get real."

Julian said, "Instead, *he* wound up trying to make *me* feel better."

Megan said, "Then maybe you got him to take his mind off what's going on. For a few minutes, anyway. Lighten up, bro. One minute you're down on Grady and your team, and the next minute you're giving yourself all this grief. Do yourself a favor — cut it out."

Julian shrugged. "I don't know how."

"You're not the guy in the hospital," said Megan. "You're the star athlete who's healthy and has a big future. You might want to think about that for a while instead of looking for things to gripe about."

When Julian left for school a few minutes later, he decided that Megan couldn't understand what he was going through. It seemed as though no one could.

Julian spent the morning unable to focus on what was happening in class. He split his time between wishing he didn't have to deal with the routine of practice and being hassled by Grady and the coach, and feeling guilty for not having been more upbeat with Barry. During English class, he imagined himself lying in bed, facing surgery, never being able to play ball again, until his teacher had to warn him about daydreaming.

When lunchtime rolled around, Julian thought he'd go outside and find a quiet place to sit by himself. He headed for the baseball field and sat on a bench nearby. Was Megan right? Could he turn his mood around? How?

"Hey," called a voice, and Julian looked up, startled.

Three boys were coming toward him. Julian wasn't happy when he recognized Grady, Mick, and Len.

"Hi," Mick said, looking nervous about what Julian's reaction would be. Len nodded.

"You want company?" Grady asked when the trio got closer. "I mean, if you'd rather be left alone, that's cool, but we'll sit with you if that's all right."

Julian's first impulse was to tell them all to leave him alone, but he remembered Barry's request. "Actually, I'd like to talk to Grady, okay? Do you guys mind?"

"Sure," said Len, looking puzzled. "See you later."

"Later," said Mick as he turned and walked away with Len. Julian watched them talk to each other as they went. Probably, he figured, they were talking about him and what a pain he was.

Grady said, "I don't get it. What is your problem with those guys? What did they do to make you not like them? What did *I* do?"

"They didn't do anything," replied Julian. "It's not that I don't like them; I just don't know them. Is that all right with you?"

"Sure, whatever." Grady pointed at himself with his thumb. "What about me? What did I do? I thought we were friends."

"Me, too." Julian couldn't believe how unfair Grady was. "I thought we were friends, too. But all you want to do is lecture me and hassle me. I should do this, I shouldn't do that, I'm not a team player. And you'd rather spend your time with those guys than with me. *I'm* not the one who's not being a friend."

"You never say anything nice to the new players," Grady insisted. "You avoid them, and when I'm with them, you avoid me. Yesterday, you wouldn't even go with me to visit Barry in the hospital. How lame is that?"

"I *did* visit him," snapped Julian. "I went last night, okay? I saw him, and we talked. But you're right, he's in pretty bad shape, I guess."

The boys said nothing for a moment, both of them thinking about Barry.

"He might not be able to play basketball again," Grady said softly.

"Yeah." Julian turned to Grady, his anger forgotten for the moment. "What would you do if it was you?"

Grady shook his head. "I don't know."

"Maybe Coach Valenti will have news about what's going on," Julian suggested.

"I don't know. It's probably too soon to know much."

Grady unwrapped his lunch. "Anyway, I'm not lecturing you."

"Yes, you are," Julian answered. "Telling me what I should do or not do — that's the coach's job, not yours."

After a pause, Grady said, "You're right. I shouldn't do that. I'm sorry; I was out of line. I won't do it anymore."

Julian wasn't expecting Grady's response. He had been ready for more arguing.

"But the coach won't let you get away with anything," Grady added. "You know he'll be all over you if you don't get it together."

Julian wanted to disagree, but couldn't. Grady was right; Coach Valenti had warned Julian already. But Julian wasn't going to say so to Grady. "That's between me and the coach," he said at last.

"Okay," Grady said. "And listen, I still want to be your friend. But don't expect me not to be friends with Mick and Len, or anyone else. We're all going to be practicing and playing together, so we might as well get along."

"Okay," Julian said, still not really happy with the idea. "Oh, one other thing. Barry asked if you and me could visit him together. He said he'd like that."

"Sure. I'd like that," Grady said. "If it's all right with you."

"Yeah, why not?" Julian said. He realized that he hadn't eaten his lunch, but he no longer felt hungry. "I better go."

"See you at practice," Grady said.

"Right." Julian wished he could make himself look forward to it.

Practice began with the usual warm-ups. In the layup drill, Julian didn't have to work too hard and made just about all his shots, going in and rising effortlessly, then banking the ball in. Once or twice, for variety, he used a finger roll to loft the ball on a high arc and through the hoop. He was one of the few boys his age who could do such a move with success.

But while Julian could look good on layups, even while not working hard, if he loafed when going for the ball after another player's shot, it showed. After one halfhearted attempt at a block, Coach Valenti called out, "Julian!"

The coach beckoned him. Julian, nervous that he'd pushed his luck too far, trotted over.

"I can see you're tired," Coach Valenti said. "So I'll

give you two choices. Number one: sit down on that bench for a few minutes, then come back ready to hustle. Number two: go to the locker room, change clothes, and go home. And don't come back until you think you're ready to play. Which is it going to be?"

Julian said, "I'll pick it up, Coach. Really."

The coach gestured to the bench. "Sit down and think about it. Go on."

Feeling every eye on him, Julian sat down on the bench. He was seething but couldn't decide whether he was angry at himself or at everybody else. A few minutes later, the coach blew his whistle to get the team together and signaled for Julian to join them.

"No more of this lounging around," he said quietly to Julian. "I mean that." He raised his voice so the whole team could hear him. "All right, we're going to do a three-on-three half-court passing exercise. The three on offense will inbound the ball at midcourt and try to score. Before you shoot, however, you have to pass the ball at least five times. After a made shot, the other team puts the ball in play from midcourt. On a missed shot, whichever team gets the rebound has to pass the ball out to midcourt, and we start again. The team with the ball has to make five passes before shooting. Any questions?"

Grady and Julian were on the first squad with the ball, along with a forward named Warren. Warren had been on the team the previous year but had seen little playing time. Mick and Len were on the defense squad, along with another new guy, a tall, skinny center named Cal.

Grady inbounded to Julian, who backed the ball in toward the basket, with Cal trying to block his move. Julian was bigger than Cal and could have turned and shot. But the drill called for five passes. So Julian faked to his right side, turned the other way, and threw a bounce pass to Warren, who was standing in the left corner near the baseline. Warren flicked a chest pass to Grady, who had managed to get away from Len behind the key. Grady threw a high pass to Julian. Julian fired the ball straight back to Grady and slid in toward the basket. Cal tried to block the lane, planting himself behind Julian's inside shoulder. But Julian wheeled away to the baseline, and Grady found him with a soft, arching pass. Cal lunged desperately to keep Julian from shooting, but Julian put up a baseline shot that swished through the net.

"All right!" said Grady.

Julian found himself grinning. This was the way it

should be. But the other squad now put the ball in play from midcourt, and Julian had to guard Cal. Though Julian had a few inches on the thinner boy, Cal proved to be surprisingly quick on his feet. He worked free to take a pass from Mick. Cal dropped a bounce pass behind him to Len and drifted inside. Len lobbed the ball to Cal, who fired it back to Len. Len bounced it to Mick, who had an open shot from fifteen feet. Julian launched himself toward him, hands extended to block a shot. But instead of shooting, Mick threw a well-timed pass to Cal. Unguarded, Cal dropped in an easy layup.

Julian knew right away that he'd made a mistake — he'd left his man free for an easy bucket to try to block a low-percentage outside shot. The coach whistled play to a stop. "What happened?" he asked Julian.

"I should have stayed with my man inside instead of worrying about the long jumper," Julian said. "I shouldn't give him the high-percentage shot."

"Good," said the coach. "That's how we learn. Okay, back to work."

A minute later, after Warren had missed a ten-foot jumper, Mick took a crosscourt pass from Len and went up for his own jump shot. Julian jumped, stretched out an arm, and just managed to get a couple of finger-tips on the ball, spoiling a good shot opportunity.

"Nice move, Julian," the coach called. "Let's have some other people on the floor."

When Julian went to the sideline, Grady turned and said, "Nice block."

Julian wiped his face with a towel. "Good assist back there."

It was almost like last year.

A few minutes later, the coach told the team to relax and left the gym for a minute. When he returned, he said, "Can I have your attention? I thought you'd want to know that Barry Streeter had his surgery earlier today. His father says it went well, but there's still no word on what happens next. Tomorrow's Saturday, and he'll be ready for company. We don't practice until midafter-noon, so you have time to drop by if you want to."

Julian and Grady exchanged looks.

"Want to go?" Julian asked.

"Absolutely," Grady replied.

Julian said, "He's going to be fine. You'll see." He wished he felt as sure as he sounded.

8

The next morning, Julian and Grady were on their way down the hall toward Barry's room when someone called Julian's name. Mrs. Streeter waved to them from the visitors' lounge. She stood up and hugged each of them in turn. She looked very tired.

"Barry will be happy to see you," she said. "Sit down. They only let in two visitors at a time, and Barry's dad and Coach Valenti are in there. But they'll be out soon."

"How is he?" asked Grady.

Mrs. Streeter sat back down with a sigh. "He's doing well, all things considered. He'll be out of the hospital tomorrow, and he'll begin physical therapy in a few days."

"That's great," Julian said.

She smiled. "He keeps talking about how he wishes he could play ball."

"We really miss him, too," said Julian.

Grady nodded. "But the main thing is, he's going to get better, right?"

Before Mrs. Streeter could reply, the coach and Mr. Streeter walked into the lounge.

"Hey, boys, glad you're here," Mr. Streeter said, shaking their hands. There were dark circles under his eyes, and he sat next to his wife and took her hand.

"Good to see you," said the coach. He looked as if he hadn't had much sleep either.

"We hear Barry's okay," said Grady.

"The doctors sound more encouraging than yesterday," answered Mr. Streeter. "Barry's going to have some tough months ahead of him. But if he works hard with the therapist, he should be fine. Why don't you go in and see him?"

Julian and Grady started out, but Mrs. Streeter called, "Don't stay too long, boys. He needs plenty of rest, and there'll be a lot of friends and relatives stopping by today."

"We'll make it quick," Julian promised.

Grady knocked on Barry's open door, and he and

Julian went inside. Barry was sitting in a wheelchair, with his injured leg propped up in front of him. He no longer had an IV in his arm, and his dressings were smaller.

"Hey, guys," Barry said, sounding as if he'd just woken up out of a deep sleep. "What's happening? Sit down."

Julian was determined to be cheerful this visit. He pulled out a chair and sat. "Practice is at four on Monday, dude. And you better be on time."

Barry smiled. "Right. Listen, if I sound a little fuzzy, it's because I just took a pain pill."

"It hurts a lot, huh?" asked Grady.

"Not as bad as yesterday," Barry replied, making a face at the memory. "But at least I'm going home."

Julian said, "I hear you'll be doing physical therapy soon."

"I start Wednesday. I met the guy this morning. He looks even tougher than the coach. It won't be fun, but he says it'll be worth it."

"Sure it will," Julian said. "Does that mean you'll be able to play again . . . sometime?"

"Probably," Barry said. "I guarantee one thing — if working hard makes any difference, then I'll play again for sure. Anyway, it's good to see you two here together."

Grady and Julian looked at each other. Julian said, "I should have come with Grady the other day. I was really dumb not to."

"No biggie," Grady said. "But this way, Barry doesn't have to waste much time on us."

"Good thing, too," Barry said. "My schedule is really full today. There's lunch and dinner. And that's about it."

"We'll be around to hassle you a lot while you're home," said Julian. "You'll be sick of us."

"Yeah, and I can't even run away when I get bored." Barry started to laugh and winced. "I have to remember not to laugh too hard."

"We won't make any jokes," Grady said. "And if we do, I promise they won't be funny ones."

"So, how do the Tornadoes look?" Barry asked. "I mean, I know it's early, but you think you might have a good year?"

"I don't know why not," Grady said.

"Too soon to tell," said Julian.

"The coach thinks you have some real talent," said Barry. "If you could only find a decent center and a point guard, you might have a fantastic season."

His friends smiled.

"I'm going to go to all your games," Barry said, "so you better be good."

Grady grinned. "If we lose, it'll be your fault for making us nervous."

Mr. Streeter stuck his head in the door. "Excuse me, some other people are waiting to see Barry, so if you boys could wrap it up . . ."

Julian stood up. "We were just leaving."

"Yeah," said Grady. "We know when we're not wanted."

"Later, guys," Barry said. "Thanks for coming. And thanks for coming together. I appreciate it."

"You should," Grady said. "You think I *like* hanging out with this doofus?"

Julian gave Grady a mock glare. "Try to pretend you like it. Like I do."

"I told you two not to make me laugh," protested Barry.

Julian was feeling a lot better about Barry and about himself when the boys returned to the visitors' lounge. Mick and Len were there, waiting to visit Barry.

"Hey," Mick said. "The coach and Barry's folks went out for a while. How's Barry doing?"

"Pretty good," said Grady. "He'll be glad to see you."

As Len and Mick got up, Julian said, "Uh, after you see him, do you guys feel like getting something to eat before practice?"

Mick looked surprised, and then pleased. "Yeah, that'd be great."

Grady said, "We'll wait for you and talk about it when you're done."

Len nodded. "Sounds good."

After Mick and Len left, Grady turned to Julian. "Wow. You were actually nice to them. You feeling okay?"

Julian sat down on a couch and looked up at Grady. "Sure. I'm just being a team leader and making sure that my teammates eat their lunch."

From the hospital, the four boys went to a nearby fast-food place for burgers. As they unwrapped their food, Len said, "What does he have to do for physical therapy, does anybody know?"

"I don't have a clue," said Grady, picking up his shake.

Julian nibbled on a French fry. "All I know is it sounds like it won't be fun."

"My cousin hurt his leg skiing," said Mick. "He was

in PT for three months. He said it was really tough, especially for the first month or so. And the therapist was, like, *really* in his face about not letting up, working through the pain and all that stuff. Cousin Donny says that for a while he didn't think it was worth going through it, but he kept at it, and later he was happy the therapist wouldn't let him quit."

"What kinds of things did he have to do?" Julian asked.

"Exercises to build up his leg muscles and keep the joints from getting all tight. Stretching for flexibility, leg lifts, exercises for his hip and his knee, a lot of stuff. Even with light weights, it was really bad at first, but the therapist made him stay with it, and his leg is normal now."

Len whistled. "Man."

"Barry'll do it," Grady said. "He's tough enough."

Julian wondered how he'd manage if it happened to him. He hoped he'd be tough enough, too. Barry's situation was giving him some food for thought.

They arrived at the gym early for practice. Julian changed quickly and went out on the court to work on his free throws. Last year, he'd spent a half hour every day shooting from the free-throw line, but he hadn't felt like doing it yet this year. Shooting free throws can be pretty monotonous, after all. But Julian decided that he would put in half an hour a day from now on.

The other three joined him and worked on different phases of their own game. Grady was trying to improve his left-handed dribbling. Len practiced outside jump shots from different spots around the key. Mick started throwing up hook shots, launching himself off his left foot, extending his left arm to ward off defenders, and releasing the ball from his outstretched right hand.

"Pretty smooth shot," Julian said after watching Mick sink one.

Mick smiled. "Thanks; sometimes it's on, and sometimes it's off. You ever shoot hook shots? You'd be tough to stop. You have the hands for it, too."

"I should work on it more," admitted Julian. "Last year, I mostly shot jumpers and layups."

Other players had drifted in and were loosening up as practice time got closer.

Mick handed Julian a ball. "Try a hook shot. Let's see how it looks."

Julian took the ball and looked up at the basket. He was just to the left of the key, about ten feet from the hoop. He dribbled once and took a step to his right, turning to bring his left shoulder toward the basket. Jumping off his left foot, he extended his left arm for balance and threw up a shot. The ball hit the front rim and caromed off.

"Great," he said. "That was pretty bad."

"You need to loft the ball more, get more arch into the shot," Mick said, flipping the ball back to Julian.

Coach Valenti's whistle echoed through the gym, and the players got ready to work.

The coach said, "We have a week before we open the season against the Falcons, and we're going to spend more time from here on doing intrasquad scrimmages. The Falcons were a pretty good team last year, and almost all their players are back this time around, so we've got our work cut out for us. But let's do some stretches, and then we'll start just like we always do, with layups."

When the Tornadoes got in line for a layup drill, Julian felt pretty good. Layup drills weren't fun, but they could be useful. He knew he needed to work on his passing. He was the first man in line to set up the shooters. When Warren, at the head of the shooting line, went in with the ball, Julian set himself, watching as Warren's shot hit the backboard too hard, clanged off the rim, and bounced toward the right sideline. Julian darted after the ball, grabbed it while it was still barely on the court, and threw a bounce pass to Cal, who caught it in midstride to go in for his layup. Cal gave him a grin as Julian trotted to the end of the shooting line.

When Julian got to the front of the line, Grady was there to feed him the ball. Grady flipped a high pass that Julian snapped up as he took off from his right foot. He put the shot in off the glass and didn't pause to look, heading straight for the other line. When his turn came again to pass to a teammate, he pulled the ball down just after it went through the netting and lobbed it gently to Mick, who caught it on the run and laid it up.

As the drill went on, Julian realized that when it was all in sync, as it seemed to be now, even a drill like this could be . . . well, maybe not fun, exactly, but definitely satisfying.

"Nice assist, Julian," called the coach. "Warren,

watch the steps there. You can get away with two steps before laying it up, but they'll get you for three."

After layups came the hated sidestep drill. The coach called it, and Julian made a face.

"Got a problem, Julian?" the coach asked.

"No problem," Julian said. "I *love* doing sidesteps."

Coach Valenti grinned. "I thought so."

The drill seemed to go on forever, but Julian was determined to stay with it until either he collapsed or the coach ended it. He faced Cal, who was probably going to be the backup center. Thin and rangy, Cal had less trouble moving from side to side than he had keeping his hands high in the proper defensive position. After a minute or so, Cal's face showed the strain, and he was gasping. Julian was feeling it, too, but he forced himself to stay with it. Cal's arms began to sag, until his hands were at waist level.

"Come on, hang in there," Julian whispered to the other boy. Cal gritted his teeth and brought his hands up again. "Not too much longer, now. That's the way! Stay tough!"

Finally, the coach clapped his hands. "All right! Take a break!"

Cal's arms flopped to his sides, and he bent over, panting. Julian wasn't feeling a whole lot better, but he leaned over to the other boy.

"You did it! You okay?"

Cal straightened out and nodded. He flexed his arms a little and bent over again.

"Very good," the coach said. "I already see an improvement in this exercise. Those of you whose arms feel like they're going to fall off, don't worry. They won't. But some of you may want to work out with light wrist weights. I keep a couple of sets in the phys. ed. office, if you want to borrow them, or you can find them at any sporting goods store. Take a couple more minutes, and then we'll get back to work."

Grady came over to Julian and said, "You remind me of a guy we had on this team last year. Always hustling, giving everything he had. He was a center, too. Let's see, what was his name again?"

Julian said, "You remind me of someone from last year, too. He was a wise guy, thought he was funny, until one of his teammates stuffed him in a basket and left him there."

"Seriously," Grady said. "What happened between last practice and now?"

Julian didn't answer right away. Then he looked Grady in the face and said, "Barry's going to be working hard, harder than he ever has, probably, just so he can come back and do these drills. How can I slack off, knowing that?"

After the break, Coach Valenti split the team into squads for a five-on-five scrimmage. Julian's squad included Grady at point guard; a stocky boy named Anthony, who had a surprisingly soft touch, at shooting guard; and Mick and Roger, another newcomer, at the forward positions. Cal would work against Julian at center for the other squad, which also included Len and a wiry guy from last year named Brandon as the guards, along with Warren and another new face, Terrell, at forward. Terrell, tall and long-armed, looked as if he had good defensive instincts.

"Julian's squad will open on offense to start," said the coach. "For the moment, I want both squads working on their zone defense. Later, you might go man-to-man instead, but we need work on our zones.

The Falcons moved the ball around well last year; they're sharp passers, and I'm thinking zones could be effective against them. I'll be calling any fouls. Okay, let's go."

Grady took the ball under his squad's basket and passed to Mick, who flipped it back to Grady to bring it into the offensive zone. Brandon, the opposing point guard, shadowed Grady to the midcourt line. The defenders went into a 2–3 zone, with the guards on either side of the key, a few feet in front of the foul line. The forwards set themselves five feet from the baseline and five feet from the sides of the key. Cal, the center, was about eight feet from the basket, to the right of the key.

Brandon moved in on Grady, who fired a chest-high pass to Roger to his left. Julian moved inside with his back to the basket. Cal slid over to pick him up. Grady came around behind Roger, who tossed him the ball and ran toward the baseline, his hands held high as if to take a pass. Terrell darted between Warren and Roger to block a pass, but Grady passed to Mick instead. Mick faked a shot and bounced a pass back to Grady as Julian pivoted around Cal toward the basket.

Grady tossed the ball too high for Cal to reach, but Julian grabbed the ball and lofted it up over the rim and into the net for two points.

As they raced back to their defensive positions, Julian and Grady touched hands briefly, congratulating each other for the bucket.

"Defense, go to a one–three–one zone," the coach called. The 1–3–1 called for Grady, as point guard, to set up in the middle near midcourt. Julian moved almost under the basket, just outside the key, while the other three defenders formed a line ten feet from the basket.

Brandon brought the ball over midcourt. Grady harassed his opponent with darting hands, trying to break his concentration and cause a turnover. Brandon gave up his dribble and held the ball overhead, looking for an open man. Grady moved in on him. Suddenly, Mick swept in, leaving Brandon trapped between two defenders and unable to dribble out of the jam. Brandon flung up a desperation pass in the general direction of Len, who was trying to get away from Anthony. Len lunged after the ball and pulled it in before it went out-of-bounds.

Len fired a chest pass to Terrell. Terrell turned to

shoot but noticed Cal, in the low post to the right of the basket, waving a hand and hoping to get the ball. Terrell threw a bounce pass to Cal, who took it and dribbled out a little farther from the key, with Julian close behind him. Warren ran to the baseline so that Cal could set a pick for him, and Cal tossed Warren the ball. Cal's pick left Warren open for a fifteen-foot jump shot, which rimmed the hoop and wouldn't fall.

Julian found himself in perfect position for the rebound. As he went up to clear the boards, he saw Grady run full-speed for the other basket, with Mick close behind. Julian threw a long, baseball-style pass that Grady caught. Len and Terrell raced back to defend as fast as they could. Len managed to catch up with Grady. Grady passed to Mick, who was racing straight up the key, and Mick laid the ball up and in.

Julian clapped his hands in appreciation of the fast-break bucket, and Coach Valenti called out, "Good hustle, Mick. Guys, look out for those breakaways. Warren, Terrell, you got caught too deep that time."

The scrimmage continued, and the defensive squads worked on different zone defenses, alternating the 2–3, 3–2, and 1–3–1. Julian especially liked the 1–3–1, which put him in great position for rebounds. But he quickly realized that Mick was a strong rebounder, too, with a talent for anticipating where to position himself to block opponents. He began to feel a little better about the Tornadoes' chances for the coming season. Terrell was a relentless defender, whose long reach could strip unwary opponents of the ball — he grabbed one away from Anthony at one point — and Cal, with a little work, could be a reliable backup at center. Cal had a good vertical leap and could shoot effectively up to twelve feet from the basket.

After fifteen minutes, Julian's squad had scored fourteen points, and their opponents had ten. The coach ended the scrimmage at that point.

"Good work!" Coach Valenti said. "I like the way you're all hustling, and I didn't see many mental errors. Anthony, try not to rush your shots. Get your feet under you and square up your shoulders before you shoot. Unless the shot clock is running down, there's no reason to hurry. But you made a nice touch pass to set up Roger's last shot. Quick ball movement usually means open shots, sooner or later.

"I saw two nice trap plays. Grady, Mick, you almost created a turnover. Brandon and Warren, good trap on Grady. Always be on the lookout for trapping defenses, guys. Be ready to help if you see a teammate getting trapped.

"Julian. Good work. But watch the elbows when you rebound. You might have got whistled for an elbow on Terrell. We don't want you getting into foul trouble. And, all of you, don't dribble so high. Some of you like to let the ball come way up, chest high or more. It's harder to control and easier to steal. Keep the dribbling lower. And dribbling should mostly involve your fingers and your wrist. Again, it's easier to control that way.

"Now, let's see each of you take a few foul shots so I can check your form. We won't use much practice time on them, so you should work on foul shots on your own."

Julian missed his first two attempts from the line. "Too flat," said the coach. "Try putting more loft on them."

He hit two out of his next three.

"Better," said Coach Valenti.

Grady went to the line, stared at the rim, and bounced the ball six times. His shot rattled around the rim and went in.

"As a rule," said the coach, "I don't like all that ball-bouncing on the free-throw line. It may throw your concentration off. More important, when you shoot, bend your knees and put more of your body into the shot. Try it again, Grady."

Grady hit two straight.

After everyone had taken a turn at the line, the coach said, "All right, we'll run another scrimmage in a little while. Take a minute to think about what you need to work on."

Mick walked up to Julian, who was trying a few more foul shots. After Julian had shot, Mick said, "I like Coach Valenti. My old coach was into 'rah-rah' stuff, but he never spent much time working on technique."

Grady came up in time to overhear this. "Yeah, you're right. The coach really gives good tips on style. He's good on height, too."

Mick stared at Grady. "Huh?"

Grady nodded, straight-faced. "Sure. When he started working with Julian, Julian was only five-three. And look at him now."

Julian said, "Yeah. I do height exercises every night. I tie weights to my feet and hang by my hands from my closet door."

Mick's laugh was loud enough to make heads turn in

his direction. He started to explain, "Grady says . . . he says that . . . he says the coach . . ."

He burst out laughing again.

Grady spread his hands and shrugged. "I didn't say anything. He just started laughing like that for no reason."

"It's all right," Julian said, pointing to Mick. "I don't think he's dangerous. He's just a little . . . weird, that's all."

The coach came back out on the floor, clapping his hands. "Let's run another scrimmage. This time, we'll focus on passing."

He rearranged the squads. Now Julian's team consisted of Len, Roger, Terrell, and Brandon. Grady, Anthony, Mick, Cal, and Warren made up the other group.

"This time, use man-to-man defense and make five passes before taking a shot," said Coach Valenti. "Keep the passes quick, move without the ball, and remember: whether you're on offense or defense, always know where the ball is. Keep those heads on swivels! Grady, put the ball in play."

Grady's squad took the ball into the offensive zone and passed it around the perimeter. Julian worked hard to keep Cal from getting easy shots from under the basket. Then Anthony got away from Len long enough to sink a fifteen-foot jump shot.

As his squad went over to offense, Julian thought he had a fast-break opportunity — but then he remembered that the team had to make five passes before shooting. So he decided not to waste his energy racing down the court. A minute later, he crossed through the key and took a bounce pass from Roger that somehow got between Grady and Mick. It was the fifth pass. Julian pivoted and jumped, his arm cocked for a shot. But when two defenders leaped toward him to try to block it, he threw a pass to Terrell instead. Terrell's shot was too hard off the board, but Julian soared high to pull down the rebound and put it back up for two points. The coach, acting as referee, blew his whistle.

"Cal, you were all over Julian on that shot. Julian, to the line for a free throw."

Julian went to the line, took a deep breath, and remembered to arch his shot more. He sank it to complete a three-point play.

Everyone played hard in the scrimmage. Mick got hot and hit three straight jumpers. Mick's squad wound up with seventeen points to fifteen for Julian's group.

Finally, the coach called it quits. "Good work, everyone! Okay, take it easy till Monday. We have a few more practices before we play the Falcons Friday afternoon. I think we'll be ready to give them a game. Julian, can I see you for a bit?"

Julian turned to Grady. "What'd I do now?" he whispered.

Grady shrugged. "Don't sweat it. You did great today. See you in the locker room."

Julian walked over to the coach, who was making notes on a clipboard. "Just a sec," the coach said.

Finally, he stuck the clipboard under his arm. "I'd been worried about you last week, but today you looked like the player I remember from last year. I just wanted you to know that I'm happy to see that guy back with us."

Julian felt a flood of relief. "Thanks."

"It makes my job easier when a veteran on the team sets a good example. I appreciate it."

Julian smiled, and the coach smiled back.

"Okay, then. Take off. Have a nice Sunday."

Julian thought he probably would.

On Sunday mornings, Mr. Pryce always made waffles for breakfast. Julian realized that he was starving as soon as he smelled the waffles and sausages from his bedroom. He raced downstairs to find the rest of his family already digging in.

"Hey, bro," said Megan, who was pouring syrup on her plate. "How's the team looking? Still awful?"

Julian speared a couple of waffles and reached for the butter. "Nope. They're looking pretty good. Don't hog the syrup."

Megan passed her brother the pitcher. "No kidding? What happened? Did you get some replacements? Or did the guys you said were terrible suddenly become superstars?"

Julian smiled. "Okay, I was wrong about the team. I made a mistake. Satisfied?"

"Hey, if you're satisfied, I'm satisfied." Megan shoved the platter of sausages closer to Julian's side of the table. "Does this mean it's okay for us to go to the games? You don't want us to stay home?"

Mr. Pryce turned around from the counter, where he was pouring more batter into the waffle iron. "Megan . . ."

"It's okay, Dad," Julian said. "When Megan's right, she's right. Not that it happens often . . . but this time, she was. I was making a big deal out of nothing. The team probably won't be as good as last year's, but it's going to be okay. And the new guys are cool."

"Is everything all right between you and Grady?" asked Mrs. Pryce.

"Sure," Julian said. "Barry helped to straighten that out. He made us come visit him together, and that was all it took, really."

"How is Barry?" Megan asked. "Is he coming home soon?"

"I think he's coming home today," Julian said. He explained what he'd heard about Barry's physical therapy. Megan winced.

"Wow! That sounds pretty heavy. And he'll have to do this therapy for how long?"

Julian cut off a piece of waffle. "A few months, they say. It sounds tough, but Barry is a tough guy. He'll do what he has to do. Anyway, after hearing about physical therapy, it seemed pretty lame to be whining about basketball practice and maybe losing some games."

"But once the therapy is over, will he be able to play again?" asked Mrs. Pryce.

Julian looked up from his last bite of sausage. "They don't know for sure, but probably. He'll give it his best shot. I'm going to call his house later, see if he's home and if he wants company." He grabbed the syrup again.

"Julian!" said Mrs. Pryce. "How can you pour so much syrup on that waffle?"

Julian grinned at his mother. "It's all in the way you use your wrist, Mom. Otherwise, you don't get a controlled stream from the pitcher."

Julian called the Streeters just after noon. Mr. Streeter said that Barry was home and would be happy to have company. Just as Julian put down the receiver, the phone rang.

"Hello?"

"Hey, Jools, it's Grady. Barry's home."

"Yeah, I talked to his father. I'm going over in a while."

"Me too. Hey, there's a good NBA game on the tube. Maybe we can watch."

"Cool. See you there."

Half an hour later, Julian found Barry and Grady in the Streeters' living room. Grady sat in an armchair, with a big bowl of chips in front of him. Barry was in a wheelchair, with his injured leg propped up. He looked tired, and Grady gave Julian a look that was meant to send Julian a message, but Julian didn't understand.

"Hey, good to see you home," Julian said, reaching out a hand for Barry to shake. Barry looked at it as if he didn't know what it meant, but finally he reached out his own hand. His shake was brief and unenthusiastic. Julian sat down and said, "It must feel great to be out of the hospital, huh?"

Barry nodded. "Yeah, pretty good. Uh, you want anything? Something to drink?" His voice was flat. Something wasn't right.

"Not right now," Julian said. "I pigged out on waffles a while ago, and I'm totally stuffed. Maybe later."

"Okay," Barry said. Julian sneaked a glance at Grady, who gave a tiny shake of his head. What was going on?

"Listen, I'll be right back," Barry said, and he slowly wheeled himself out of the room.

Julian and Grady watched him go, and when he was out of sight, Julian leaned closer to Grady and whispered, "What's happening? Does he feel sick or something?"

Grady shook his head and, keeping his voice low, replied, "I don't know. He's been, like, totally down since I got here. Won't say anything, won't do anything. I don't know. Maybe we should go."

Julian frowned. "Did his mom or dad say anything?"

"Nope. I mean, they said they're glad to see me and they're happy that Barry's home, but they didn't say there was anything wrong."

Julian wasn't sure what to do. "Let's see what happens. Maybe he'll lighten up, or tell us what's going on."

The boys sat there quietly until Barry returned and wheeled himself back to where he had been sitting.

"Sorry," he said.

There was an embarrassing silence that Julian finally broke. "Did Grady tell you? We had a really good practice yesterday."

"That right?" Barry asked, not sounding like he cared much either way. "Good deal."

Grady said, "Maybe Barry doesn't want to hear about us playing hoops right now."

Barry said, "No, that's okay. I don't mind."

Julian noticed a pair of crutches leaning in a corner. "How good are you with those crutches? Is it tough getting around with them?"

"A little," Barry said. "I have to get used to them."

Mr. Streeter came in. "Julian, glad you could make it. Can I get you boys anything? Are you hungry, thirsty?"

"No, thanks," said Julian.

"I'm fine," Grady said.

Barry just shook his head.

"Well, if there's anything I can do, just holler," said Barry's father. He looked at his son for a moment and left the room.

There was another silence. Grady finally said, "Look, Barry, if you'd rather not have company right now, that's cool. We don't have to stick around."

"No, really. Don't leave." Barry took a deep breath. "It may not sound like it, but I'm glad you came over."

"Okay," said Julian. "It's just that you seem down,

and if you feel sick, or you got bad news or something, or if you want to talk about anything, that's okay."

"Or you don't have to, you know, if you'd rather not," added Grady. "But yesterday, you were, like, really happy, and today, well . . ."

Barry leaned back and closed his eyes. "This whole thing has been like a roller coaster. Way up, and then way down.

"At first it was, 'Wow, I could've been killed in the accident; I'm lucky.' Then they said, 'You need this operation,' which was scary, but I got through it. But then I heard them tell my parents that they weren't sure I'd walk without crutches ever again."

"Wow, that must have been . . ." Julian trailed off, unable to imagine what it would have been like.

Barry nodded. "Yeah, but then they operated, and afterward this doctor says, 'You'll need crutches for a while, but not for long, and you should be walking without them in a couple of months.' So I was feeling great about that, and that was when I saw you guys yesterday.

"But this morning, before they let me go home, they said they don't know yet if my knee will ever be able to handle what they call 'high-impact' stuff. Like basketball. So now I'm looking at that, plus this therapy, which isn't going to be any fun at all. If I sound down, that's why."

"I can see how it would get to you," Grady said. "Not knowing what will happen."

"Well, I know that therapy will happen," Barry said. "And it makes me nervous, I guess."

Julian said, "I'd feel the same way."

Barry smiled. "But it's good to talk to someone about this. Sure, I can talk to my folks, but I don't want them upset, which they would be if I tell them how nervous I am."

"I bet they're upset anyway," said Grady. "But, yeah, I know what you mean."

Barry shrugged. "Hey, whatever will happen, will happen, but sometimes it gets to me."

Julian hitched himself forward and looked Barry in the eyes. "I bet you'll handle the therapy fine. And I bet you'll play ball again, too. That's what I think. And you know we'll be there for you any way we can."

"Absolutely," said Grady.

Barry said, "You guys are great."

"You helped us," Julian said, "and we'll be there for you."

Barry blinked. "Helped you?"

Julian looked at his hands. "When I heard that Max was gone and you were hurt," he said quietly, "and I was the only starter left from last year, it messed me up. I was all, 'The team is going to be terrible,' and 'I'll look bad,' and stuff like that.

"But you turned me around. Seeing you in the hospital, I understood that I was being a jerk, complaining about my little problems. And then you made Grady and me visit you together and work it all out. That's how you helped me."

Barry said, "I didn't really do anything."

"Sure you did," Julian insisted. "And we're going to help you. We'll be with you all the way. We'll see that you don't even think about giving up on yourself."

"Right!" Grady agreed. "Before you're finished with your therapy, you're going to be sick of us. But we'll be there anyway."

"And you'll do what you have to," said Julian.

Barry didn't say anything for a moment. Then he nodded. "I guess I will."

"So that's that," said Grady. "Um . . . I think that NBA game may have started. And did I hear someone offering something to drink?"

11

Practices went on, and the Tornadoes geared up for the game against the Falcons. On Wednesday, Coach Valenti put in a new play that he thought might work for either Len or Anthony, the two best outside shooters among the guards.

"It's a double screen," he explained, drawing a diagram on his clipboard. "The center — Julian or Cal — has the ball, and a forward, like you Mick, moves up next to him, here or here." He pointed to spots just outside the foul line and five feet from the key. "The shooting guard uses the double screen to get loose from his defender, takes the ball from the center, and shoots from fifteen feet.

"We can also use the same setup to start a pick-and-roll, with the center pivoting and going to the basket. Any questions?"

"Will this work against a zone?" asked Grady.

"It should work against either a zone or a man defense," the coach replied. "If they're playing man-to-man, the screen picks off the defender. If they use a zone, we flood the zone, and someone should be open. Either way, it could be effective. Let's work on it. Julian, you're the center. Mick, you set the screen with him. Len, you're the shooter. Then we'll try it as a pick-and-roll."

The three players ran it by themselves first, and Len banked in the shot.

"Good. Cal, Terrell, and Anthony, go in on defense," said the coach.

Though the double screen gave Len the open shot, the shot missed, and Cal pulled down the rebound when Julian reacted too slowly.

Coach Valenti said, "Julian, when the ball leaves Len's hands, slide across the key while Mick moves closer to the baseline. Look to block out. Try it again."

After a few more times, the coach had them try the pick-and-roll version of the play, and then had the offensive trio switch with the defenders so that they could learn the play.

Finally, Coach Valenti said, "Good. Let's move on.

Before we scrimmage, time for a sidestep drill. Julian, did you say something?"

Julian put on his most innocent look. "I was only saying how much I love this drill."

The coach smiled. "That's what I thought. Okay, set up!"

After the drill, the coach set up the scrimmage. "Today, I want to try moving from man defense to zone on my signal. Most of the Falcons have worked together for more than a full season; I want to try to rattle them a little and maybe catch them off guard. You boys who played them last year should remember how good their passing game is."

Julian was teamed with Grady, Len, Mick, and Warren. They started on defense, and the coach signaled them to use a 1–3–1 zone. Brandon brought the ball across the midcourt line, and Grady picked him up. Julian moved down close to the basket, guarding Cal, who settled into the low post just to the right of the key. Brandon fired a hard pass to Roger, who dribbled twice, faked a pass inside, and tossed back to Brandon. Cal kept moving without the ball, shifting back and forth across the key, darting outside, then backing up toward the baseline. Julian stayed between Cal and the basket, making sure he knew where the ball was at all times as it was passed around.

Terrell took a pass from Anthony, quickly flipped the ball to Brandon, and came up next to Cal to set up a double screen. Brandon threw a pass to Cal, whose back was to the basket, and Anthony came up behind the screen. Cal threw Anthony the ball. Len, trying to guard Anthony, couldn't get through Cal and Terrell.

Cal suddenly turned toward the basket, and Julian recognized the pick-and-roll being set up. Instead of staying with Cal, he took a step toward Anthony and leaped high, arms extended, deflecting Anthony's pass and then catching the ball. Len immediately broke for the other basket, followed quickly by Mick and Warren. Julian threw the ball to half-court, where Mick took it in full stride. Running as fast as he could, Roger caught up to Mick and tried to poke the ball away. Mick passed to Warren, running to his right. Warren stopped short, ten feet from the basket, and put up a shot that went around the rim and off. Mick was able to grab it and put it through the hoop.

Brandon's squad scored on its next possession, when Anthony got open against a 3–2 zone and hit a short jumper. Julian got the two points back only fifteen seconds later, taking a beautiful feed from Grady and laying the ball in. At the end of five minutes, Julian felt as if he'd played almost a full game; the end-to-end action had been that intense. He wasn't even sure which squad had scored the most points.

"Good work, everyone!" the coach called. "Take a breather while I mention a few things."

The coach pointed out areas to improve, then held up one finger. "One more session before we play the Falcons on Friday. You've made a lot of progress, and I want you to keep it up! Get your rest and work on your free throws. See you tomorrow."

As they changed into street clothes, Grady tapped Julian's shoulder. "Wasn't today Barry's first therapy session? I wonder how it went."

"We could call and find out," Julian suggested.

"Or we could ride over there and ask him," said Grady. "We both have our bikes."

Julian had called Barry every day but had not seen him since the weekend.

As they rode, Grady said, "I hope it wasn't too bad."

Julian, who had been thinking the same thing, nodded.

When they rang the bell at the Streeter house, Barry's mother answered. "Hi, boys. Come on in. I'll tell Barry you're here."

"How did it go today?" asked Grady.

"I'll let him tell you himself," said Mrs. Streeter. "I'll be right back."

She came back a moment later. "Barry is out back. Go right on through."

The boys went through the kitchen and out the back door. Barry was sitting on the patio in a lounge chair, his crutches propped up against a nearby table. He turned around and said, "Hey, guys. Pull up those chairs."

As he grabbed a chair, Julian asked, "How was it?"

Barry waited for his visitors to sit. He looked a little pale, Julian thought, but then, Barry hadn't been outside much lately.

"It was about what I was told it'd be," Barry said. "Bad."

"Really?" Grady said.

"Let's put it this way," said Barry, shifting his position in the chair with a noticeable effort. "It was tougher than the worst practice session I ever had. This therapist — his name's Sean — doesn't let up. We did all this stuff with my leg, with weights, without weights. I was totally wiped out afterward. But . . ."

He paused for a long moment, until Julian couldn't stand it any longer.

"Yeah? But *what*?"

Barry smiled for the first time since their arrival. "But . . . I *did* it! I was afraid I'd give up, or have to quit or something. But everything he told me to do, I did. And Sean was satisfied. He said I did good work."

"All *right*!" Julian pumped a fist in the air. "That must have felt great!"

Barry said, "It really did. I didn't know what to expect, except that it would be rough. And it *was* rough. But I did it! And now I know I'll be able to do it tomorrow, too. It won't get easier, because Sean'll want me to do more reps, use more weight, and so on. But I know that whatever he wants me to do, I can handle it."

"Fantastic!" said Grady. "When are you coming back to school?"

"Next Monday," Barry said.

"Are you going to make it to the game on Friday?" Julian asked. "We play the Falcons at four, at their court."

"I'll be there," Barry promised. "The Falcons moved

the ball around a lot, if I remember right. Not much height, or at least they didn't have any really tall guys last year. But they sure could pass."

Julian nodded. "That's what the coach says they'll do this year. And maybe some of them have put on some height. I mean, I'm two inches taller; some of them are probably taller, too."

"Well, anyway, I'll be there," Barry said. "And I'll stick around for the victory party."

"Whoa," Julian said, holding up both hands. "Let's not take anything for granted."

Barry laughed. "Okay, then I'll stick around for the victory party or the consolation party, whichever it is."

"Tell you what," Julian said. "Even if we lose, it's going to be a victory party for *you*."

"Cool," said Barry. "Then I get to decide what kind of pizza we have."

"It's a deal," Grady said.

Julian added, "As long as you don't get anchovies."

On Friday afternoon, a little caravan of cars drove the Tornadoes and their fans — mostly the family members who could attend — to the Falcons' home court. Julian's parents and Megan came, and Coach Valenti arranged to drive Barry. About a hundred people sat in the bleachers assigned to the Tornado rooters, while there were twice as many cheering for the home team.

As the Tornadoes changed into their black-and-gold uniforms, the coach went around talking to the players individually. To Julian he said, "Don't worry about pacing yourself too much. I'll put Cal in whenever you look like you need a breather. And you may be surprised by their starting center — he's grown quite a bit since last year."

A referee ducked his head into the room. "We'll be ready to go in five minutes."

The coach clapped his hands. "Listen up, everyone. You're ready for this game. Remember: know where the ball is at all times when you're on the floor. Talk to each other, especially on defense. Look for my signals from the bench about what defense to play. Have a good game and enjoy yourselves. Let's warm up."

Julian led the team out onto the gym floor. The Falcons, wearing light-blue uniforms trimmed in white, were already on the court as the Tornadoes started a layup drill. Julian looked for the opposing center and spotted him quickly. The guy was definitely taller, close to Julian's height.

Julian decided to focus on the warm-ups and not the opposition. After what seemed like almost no time at all, the ref blew his whistle, and the teams cleared the court. Julian saw his family sitting a couple of rows back, and Megan caught his eye and waved. Barry, in his wheelchair, was sitting in the front row near the Tornado bench. The scoreboard clock showed eight minutes, the length of a quarter.

Coach Valenti waved the team into a huddle.

"These guys are a challenge. But you can meet it. Are you ready?"

"*Yeah!*" they yelled in chorus. Down the court, a similar yell went up from the Falcons. Julian saw that the Falcons had twelve players, as opposed to the Tornadoes' ten. Not a big edge, he decided.

The ref signaled for the teams to come out. Julian, Grady, Mick, Len, and Terrell took their positions on the floor and shook hands with their opponents. Julian thought he might have an inch on the Falcon center. But his opponent was more muscular. That could be a disadvantage, however; he might tire more quickly with the extra weight.

The league had done away with the opening tip-off. Instead, the ref tossed a coin, asking Julian to call heads or tails. Julian called tails and won the toss. The Tornadoes would start on offense in the first and last quarter.

The Falcons stayed behind the midcourt line as Len inbounded the ball to Grady, who slowly dribbled down the court. As he reached the middle of the court, the Falcon point guard came out to cover him, and the Falcons moved into a man-to-man defense.

Julian went to the low post and turned his back to the basket. The Falcon center was behind his right shoulder, not giving him much room to maneuver. Mick moved outside, and Grady threw him a chest-high pass. Julian cut across the lane, his hands high as if to take a pass, but Mick bounced the ball to Len instead. Len dribbled closer to the basket, faked a shot, and fired a pass to Julian. Terrell went to the baseline behind Julian, who threw him the ball. Terrell took a jump shot that rimmed the basket but wouldn't drop. Julian outleaped two Falcons, pulled down the rebound, and saw Len break away from his man. He hit Len with a chest pass, and Len threw up a shot that swished through the net. The Tornadoes had scored first.

Coach Valenti signaled for a 1–3–1 zone as the Tornadoes hustled back to defend. The Falcon point guard dribbled into their front court, found a crease in the zone, and fired a fifteen-foot bull's-eye to tie the score. Julian made a note to tell the Tornado guards to stick close to that guy, in case that shot wasn't a fluke.

When the Tornadoes took the ball again, the Falcon center tried to intercept a pass thrown by Terrell. Len got to the ball first. Julian was free and streaked to the basket. Len saw him and threw a high pass that Julian took on his way to the hoop. As he released the ball, a Falcon forward came down hard on his arm. As the ref's whistle sounded, the shot banked in. Cheers and clapping thundered from the Tornado bleachers.

"Number four, blue," called the ref. "On the arm."

Julian walked to the free-throw line and took a deep breath. The ref bounced the ball to him, and Julian focused on the front rim. He reminded himself to keep his right elbow under the ball, bent his knees, and sank the foul shot, giving the Tornadoes a 5–2 lead.

But a minute later, the Falcon center hit a jumper from fifteen feet out. Julian realized that he would probably have to guard this guy outside, meaning that he might not be in position for some rebounds. He hoped Mick and the others could take up the slack.

Six minutes into the first quarter, Coach Valenti called time. The Falcons were ahead, 15–13. The coach gathered the team together. "All right, we're looking good, but these guys are hot from the perimeter. We need to stay tight on that little guard; he can shoot from anywhere. And the center, too. Let's stick with man-to-man for now. Cal, you're in for Julian, and Roger, take over for Terrell. Anthony, give Len

a breather. Brandon, get right in that guard's shirt."
Brandon, who had come in for Grady a minute earlier,
nodded.

But when the teams went back out, the hot-shooting
guard was on the bench. His replacement, Julian noticed, liked to dribble high. Grady nudged Julian.
"Look at that dribble. Brandon might be able to —"

Before he could finish, Brandon had flicked the ball
away from the dribbler with a lightning move. He
passed to Anthony, who sank a shot from the baseline
to tie the score.

Just before the end of the quarter, Cal was called
for a three-second violation. With ten seconds left,
the Falcon guard came back in and, just before the
buzzer, sank a shot from the back of the key. The Falcons took the lead again, 17–15.

During the second quarter, Julian came back in. He
beat the second-string Falcon center to the basket,
took a pass from Roger, and scored. The Falcons
quickly brought back their starting center, who hit another outside jump shot to put his team ahead again.
Grady leaned in toward Julian. "You need to guard
him outside." Julian nodded.

A minute later, the Falcon center swung outside to the left of the key and took a pass from a guard. Julian ran out to defend, arms high. The shot arched over his attempted block, but caromed hard off the front rim. As Grady grabbed the rebound, Julian broke for the other end of the floor, slowed down to take Grady's long pass, and banked home a layup.

As Julian trotted back on defense, he heard Barry call out, "All right, Jools!"

But in the closing minute of the first half, the Tornadoes seemed to lose their shooting touch, while the Falcon guard hung on to his. He hit two long jumpers and, when Len fouled him, converted a free throw. The buzzer ended the second quarter with the Falcons enjoying their biggest lead, 26–19.

In the locker room, Coach Valenti said, "They can't stay hot all day. Let's just play our game and not do anything foolish. Julian or Cal, you'll have to keep guarding that starting center outside. Julian, if you can hit from outside, we can get that center away from the paint on D. Then we might be able to get high-percentage shots from our forwards. We're going to start with the man-to-man defense at first in this half, but watch for my signals; we may want to change. We can win this game, guys. Take a minute to think about what we need to do, okay?"

The Falcons started the third quarter on offense, and it looked as if they wanted to give their shooting guard another chance at a long-distance basket. But this time, instead of shooting, he wheeled past Len and drove toward the hoop. Julian had been on the other side of the key, but made a quick sidestep move to block the lane. The guard rammed a shoulder into Julian, and the ref stopped play.

"That's a charge on number twelve, blue."

The Tornadoes took over, and Grady came down the court. After several passes around the perimeter, Julian, who'd stayed in the low post, darted to a spot fifteen feet from the basket and took a pass from Len. He spun around and launched a jumper. It banked off the glass and in, bringing the score to 26–21. Suddenly, the Falcons had something new to think about.

On the Falcons' next possession, Mick stepped in front of a pass meant for one of their forwards and picked it off. He threw it to Grady, and the Tornadoes headed downcourt. Again, Julian moved out from the baseline, and this time, the center followed him. Mick suddenly broke toward the basket, and Julian threw a bounce pass that caught the center by surprise. Mick laid it up and in, and was fouled in the process. He hit the free throw, and suddenly, it was a two-point game at 26–24.

It stayed very tight through the rest of the third quarter and into the fourth. Julian came out for Cal a minute into the fourth quarter, and at the same time, Anthony went in for Len. The Tornadoes took the ball and got it inside to Cal. Terrell moved next to Cal, and Julian elbowed Len, who was sitting next to him. "They're using the double screen!"

Sure enough, Anthony moved behind the two bigger players, and Cal got him the ball. Anthony's jumper went in from fifteen feet, tying the score at 34–34.

When Julian went back into the game shortly afterward, the score remained tied, and there were three minutes left in the fourth quarter. But the Falcons, using their quick passing game, were able to spring their shooting guard loose for two shots, plus a free throw, and they led by five.

A minute later, with the clock running down, Julian had the ball in the low post. The center was guarding him closely. When Julian looked around for an open player, he didn't see one. He whirled around and threw up a jumper . . . that was off target. But Mick sliced in between two Falcon rebounders and pulled down the ball. He leaped, let go a shot, and was hit on the shoulder as he did. The shot went in, and Mick went to the line for a free throw.

The Falcon fans began to yell at the top of their voices, hoping to distract him. But Mick's attention was fixed on the rim as he held the ball, flexed his knees, and put it up and in. Once more, it was a two-point game, 39–37.

As the Tornadoes raced back on defense, Julian checked the clock. There was less than a minute. Coach Valenti whistled sharply and signaled for the 1–3–1 zone defense. The Falcons passed the ball around, hoping to flood the zone, force the Tornadoes to foul, or run out the clock. With fifteen seconds to go, Len lunged just as a Falcon forward passed the ball. He deflected it away from its target, and Terrell grabbed it. The Tornadoes had fourteen seconds to score.

Coach Valenti called a time-out — the last time-out the team had. "Okay, we're going to use the double screen, but this time, we'll run the pick-and-roll. Julian, you and Terrell will be the screen, Len will fake the shot and give it back to Julian, and maybe we'll even get them to foul. Let's go!"

Julian moved into place as the fans on both sides began to roar. Grady passed to Terrell, who swung the ball around to Len on the right side. Len passed to Julian as Terrell came up to set the screen next to Julian. Len came in behind the screen, and Julian threw him the ball. There were four seconds left on the clock as Julian pivoted and moved for the basket. Len passed, throwing high so that Julian would be the only player who could reach the ball.

He threw it *too* high. The ball sailed just over Julian's fingertips and out-of-bounds. The ref stopped play with two seconds on the clock.

The Falcon rooters yelled, whistled, and clapped. A Falcon guard took the ball and threw a long pass downcourt. As a Falcon guard pulled it in, the buzzer sounded.

Final score: Falcons 39, Tornadoes 37.

Len bent over, hands on knees, looking miserable. Julian draped an arm around his shoulders. "Hey, it's okay! We gave these guys all they could handle. You played great!"

Len slowly straightened up and gave Julian a look of gratitude. "We'll get 'em next time."

"You bet!" said Julian as the players on both teams went around shaking hands.

Grady looked at Julian. "Well, we almost had them. What can you do?"

Julian smiled. "Know what? This was a great game! And that's the bottom line."

Grady thought for a second, then nodded. "Hey, Jools, when you're right, you're right."

They walked off the court together.

Matt Christopher®

Muhammad Ali	Randy Johnson
Lance Armstrong	Michael Jordan
Kobe Bryant	Peyton and Eli Manning
Jennifer Capriati	Yao Ming
Dale Earnhardt Sr.	Shaquille O'Neal
Jeff Gordon	Albert Pujols
Ken Griffey Jr.	Jackie Robinson
Mia Hamm	Alex Rodriguez
Tony Hawk	Babe Ruth
Ichiro	Curt Schilling
LeBron James	Sammy Sosa
Derek Jeter	Tiger Woods

MATT CHRISTOPHER

THE #1
SPORTS SERIES
FOR KIDS

®

Read them all!

*Previously published as Crackerjack Halfback

All available in paperback from Little, Brown and Company
**Previously published as Pressure Play
***Previously published as Baseball Pals